When Couples Play

5 Filthy Fantasies

Just One Night
Freeuse for the Night
Nurse for the Night
Used for the Night
Needing Her that Night

Lacey Cross

TWISTED ROSE
✦ PUBLISHING ✦

Contents

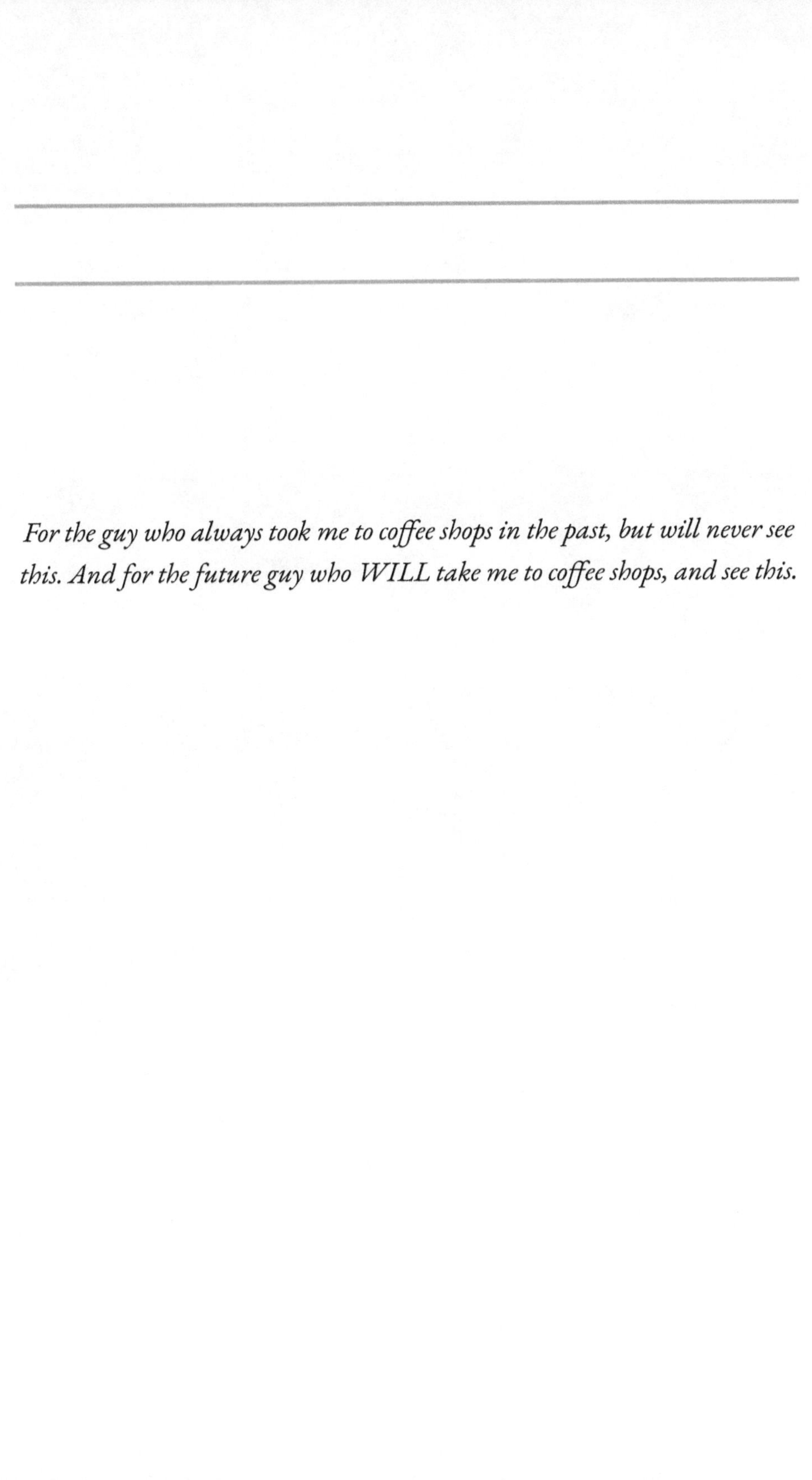

For the guy who always took me to coffee shops in the past, but will never see this. And for the future guy who WILL take me to coffee shops, and see this.

JUST ONE NIGHT

Chapter 1

When Michael entered the small coffee shop, he was already running late. Glancing around, he looked for his wife since they'd made a tentative plan to get coffee together. She'd scheduled a routine doctor's appointment and said to just have coffee without her if she wasn't there.

He didn't see her anywhere, so he ordered his latte and sat down at one of the small round tables by the window. Glancing outside, he watched rain drip from the eaves onto the wet pavement. Just another typical day in Seattle. Several couples strolled by the window, and whenever he saw an umbrella he smiled at the tourists. If you lived in the area long enough, you didn't bother with an umbrella. Besides, the misty rain always seemed to hit you sideways, and you'd be soaked with or without one.

Rainy days like this always reminded him of their wedding a little over ten years ago. They had an evening wedding, and it was wet and miserable. His wife loved banana clips that were all the rage in the mid-80s and wore a rhinestone encrusted one for their wedding. Michael's hair was in a mullet and now, whenever they look at their wedding pictures, they just laughed. Thank God mullets went out of style.

Michael's wife still hadn't shown about ten minutes later. He double-checked his watch and out of the corner of his eye he glimpsed a brunette woman in a clingy, sapphire-blue dress with a sparkly blue wrap enter the cafe. The woman looked to be in her mid-30s and had a body like his wife's — small and fit with fabulous legs. The short dress gave him an ample view of her long, lean calves and part of her upper thigh. Michael's cock stirred to life from the memory of the last time his wife's legs wrapped around his waist while he fucked her on the kitchen counter. God, that was a wonderful night. The legs of the woman who just entered the shop would wrap around him the same, and he fought the urge to stroke himself under the table.

The woman in blue waited in line to order her drink and Michael admired the way her wrap twinkled in the dim lights. A thin wrap doesn't protect much from the rain, so he figured she must have driven and parked close. When she wandered over to the tables with her mug, Michael busied himself with his drink but still kept peeking glances at her. She settled in at a small corner table across from Michael, and when she noticed him looking at her, she smiled and dipped one manicured red fingertip into her beverage to test the temperature. She gave no sign whether it was too hot, but lifted her finger to her mouth and gently sucked the tip while keeping eye contact.

The thought of her tongue on her finger got him hot and bothered, so he quickly glanced away and tried to make himself busy with his almost-finished latte. He could hear rustling around at her table, and his curiosity got the better of him as he peeked over at her again. She was removing the blue wrap and her shoulders were bare. The shadows outlined her collarbones. A small silver pendant in the shape of a heart laid in the hollow of her throat and Michael wanted to nibble and explore the column of her neck. Would she moan while he kissed and licked her smooth skin? Michael's throat was dry, and he took a sip of his latte, licking his lips as he finished the last dregs. He tried to convince himself that his dry mouth had to be from the hot drink and not the sexual daydreaming about the woman.

He continued to watch her out of the corner of his eye as she pulled out a pack of cigarettes and dug around in her small purse, obviously looking for matches. Finding none, she looked up and caught him watching. She smiled and tipped up her cigarette and nodded towards it, obviously asking if he had a light. He nodded in response. He wasn't a smoker but he always believed in being prepared, and carried a lighter on him for some million-in-one chance he ended up stranded in the woods and needed to make a fire. When Michael was a boy, his uncle spun a story about a guy who had died in the woods from lack of matches, and since then he always carried a lighter on him. His wife laughed at him for being so over-prepared, but it was one small thing that had been a habit since he was young.

The woman stood up slowly, and the fabric of her dress slipped down her thighs. The dress molded to her curves, and he envisioned how soft her skin would be. She moved to his table and bent over him while he lit her cigarette.

She took a drag on it and blew the smoke out. "Thank you, I needed that badly," she purred in a husky voice.

He wasn't sure if her voice normally sounded that way or if it was because of the smoke, but he bet she sounded fabulous moaning and whimpering.

Indicating the empty chair across from him, she queried, "You meeting someone?"

Michael glanced at his watch again. His wife had told him that if she was over twenty minutes late, he should just go home. It had been more time than that, so he knew his wife wouldn't show up.

"No, I'm not meeting anyone."

The woman smiled, showing small, even, white teeth. "Mind if I join you then? I'm a bit lonely tonight and your window table is nicer than mine."

Michael almost stumbled on his words like a foolish teenager and when he blushed, he was glad the dim lighting would hide it. "No, I'd like some company."

While the woman retrieved her purse and wrap, Michael slipped his hand under the table to remove his wedding ring and quickly pocketed it. He didn't want to talk about his wife to this beautiful stranger. It would be easier to pretend he was single and fancy free if he was ringless.

The woman came back, sat down gracefully next to him, and crossed her legs so that Michael, yet again, had an unobstructed view of her thighs.

"I'm Alyssa," the woman said while flipping her long brown hair behind her shoulder. She looked at him expectantly, and he realized she was waiting for his name.

"I'm Michael," he blurted out, and she took another drag of her cigarette and smiled around it.

"So, Michael. You married? Have kids? What do you do for a living?"

Alyssa tapped the end of her cigarette on the ashtray as she recited the list of the standard topics people use when they don't know each other. Michael looked at her and realized he didn't want their limited time together to go in that direction. He didn't want a normal meaningless conversation with a stranger in a coffee shop.

Michael leaned over, and in a low, gravelly voice told her, "The way your dress moves against your body makes me want to lift your skirt and lick you all over."

Instead of looking surprised, Alyssa's eyes took on a predatory gleam. She stamped the barely smoked cigarette in the ashtray and abandoned it.

"You know, I don't even smoke. I only did it to get your attention."

She glanced around the room, almost as if she was checking if anyone was watching. "Want to get out of here?"

Michael could barely nod as his body heated even more at the thought of what he was doing. He followed her out of the cafe and trailed behind, so that to the casual observer it didn't look like he was with her. He studied her legs as she walked. She wore black strappy sandals with three-inch heels. He could clearly see the arch of her foot and he thought about running his hands up the arch and over her calves. He was definitely a leg man.

Alyssa stopped by a dark green four-door BMW and pressed the unlock button on her key fob. Michael climbed into the passenger seat while she settled into the driver's side. She looked out the front window for a moment, not moving. He waited breathlessly, hoping she wouldn't change her mind. Finally, she turned to him and put her hand on his thigh.

"I want you to know I don't normally do this." She looked him right in the eye, and he believed her.

"I don't do this either." His breath rushed out in relief. She wasn't changing her mind.

Alyssa started the car, and they stayed silent while she drove. Michael had plenty of time to think about what he wanted to do to her. He had plans to hit a few stores after getting coffee, so no one expected him home for several hours. There was no rush and he could take his time with Alyssa.

Michael was a little surprised when she pulled into the parking lot of a prestigious downtown hotel. As they got out of the car, she explained she was only in town for tonight. Michael felt sleazy because her words relieved him, but it was simpler if she was leaving town tomorrow. A one-night stand is all he wanted.

She took his hand as they crossed the lobby and entered the elevator. She pressed the button for the 12th floor and turned to him. As the elevator doors closed, she pressed him against the back wall of the elevator while the handrail on the wall dug into his back. She slipped her hand on the back of his head, and pulled him towards her, giving him a long, violent kiss that left them both breathless. The kiss made him realize that tonight would not be the soft, sensual night he had envisioned.

Just as the elevator door opened she pulled away from him, slightly biting his lower lip while doing so. She clutched his hand again and pulled him down the corridor. The room was one of the best the hotel offered, and across the room he glimpsed a king-sized bed through a curtained French door.

Alyssa dropped her purse on a couch and slowly removed her wrap, taking the time to hang it up in the small hotel closet. Michael glimpsed the empty closet, and the only other evidence of luggage was a small carry-on bag sitting on the dresser. She must be the type who packs light.

She turned to Michael, removed his coat, and threw it on the back of an oversized chair by the bed. When Alyssa kneeled down and quickly removed his shoes, he marveled at how silky her brown hair looked and resisted the urge to run his fingers through it. Even if he had wanted to, there wouldn't have been time. Alyssa seemed determined to get down to business, and her abruptness surprised him because he had pictured them undressing each other slowly. When she finished with his shoes, she pushed him through the French doors and onto the bed.

He laid there, braced up on his elbows, enjoying the view while she removed her silver earrings and set them on the nightstand. When she lifted a leg to the bed to undo the straps on her sandals, his cock throbbed and stiffened. Just watching the muscles of her leg contract with the motion was enough to get him thinking of kissing up her inside thigh. She ditched her sandals and removed her stockings so quickly that Michael felt a little deprived of the pleasure of seeing it. He loved a good striptease.

As soon as she finished with her stockings, Alyssa pounced on him. She straddled his groin and brought her lips to his for a long, sensual kiss with plenty of tongue. His cock strained against the fabric of his jeans as she ground against him. When she slid her hands underneath his shirt, his stomach muscles jumped and he almost groaned at how good her soft hands felt. God, he shouldn't be doing this, but it was amazing.

She stopped kissing him long enough to tug on his shirt, and he lifted slightly to let her pull it off. The entire time she never let up on the pressure of grinding against him. Once he was shirtless, she started at his mouth and nibbled her way down his neck. He closed his eyes as her cool, wet tongue flicked down his chest, pausing at his nipples. Women usually ignored his nipples, but she bit on them gently and a jolt of pleasure zipped straight to his cock.

She stopped grinding against him as she moved down his body with her mouth. Her tongue flicked into his belly button once, and he opened his eyes in surprise and groaned. He was more turned on than he ever remembered being in his entire life. He was beyond caring how wrong this was. She unbuttoned his jeans, and he arched his pelvis up so she could pull them down his legs until only his cotton boxers stood between her and his cock. She grasped his shaft through the fabric and slowly rubbed him. Her soft touch drove him wild, and he tried to press harder against her hand. She only laughed at him and pulled his boxers down, exposing his package.

Once Michael was totally nude for her, she took advantage of it. Kneeling between his legs, she tickled the inside of his thighs in gentle circles,which somehow made him get even harder. Alyssa moved one finger slowly towards his cock. She touched the tip of him with just that one finger, and then drifted down the underside of his shaft until she reached the base. He loved watching her obvious pleasure as she teased him.

She purred, "What do you want?"

He opened his mouth to speak and realized he didn't care how or what she did, just as long as he fucked her soon. He chose the easiest answer. "I want you."

She flattened out her hand, grasped his balls in her palm, and gently massaged them. He moaned and almost came from the unexpected pleasure. The way she touched his body was different from anyone else he'd ever been with. All his nerve endings were alive just being close to her, and every brush of her fingers made him breathless. She shifted her body and her warm, wet mouth engulfed the tip of his cock. Her hand still massaged his balls and he thrust upward, forcing his cock deeper into her throat. Her tongue swirled all around his shaft, and spikes of pleasure coursed down to his toes. He wouldn't last much longer.

Alyssa slowly face fucked him for several strokes and then pulled his cock all the way out of her mouth. Working the other hand in tandem with her mouth, she pressed the tip of his cock against her lips before opening them and slipping him inside. As she moved her mouth down the length of him, her hand moved down also, bringing him additional pleasure. Michael, breathing heavily, fisted his hands in her hair. He suddenly knew what he wanted.

"I want to be inside you. Now!"

Alyssa stopped sucking on his cock and took her head away. The wetness of her saliva made him shiver in the cool air. On her knees beside him on the bed, she lifted her arms and pulled off her dress in one swift motion, revealing white g-string panties and matching bra. Grabbing his hand, she moved it to the back of her ass and he groaned when he encountered the band of her g-string. Maybe he could fuck her and leave her panties on? Straddling him again, she trapped his cock against her pussy and rotated her hips so he rubbed against the satin panties covering her slit.

Gliding his hands up her side, when he reached her bra strap she demanded, "Take it off."

He complied and popped the hooks loose, exposing her small, pert breasts to his view. Her breasts were the perfect size for him. He loved being able to cup the entire globe in his hand, and it was just enough to hold on to and suck.

He sat up and toyed with her nipples, rolling the hard buds between his thumb and index finger while Alyssa gasped. When he affixed his mouth to a nipple, she moaned loudly and his cock throbbed in response. Running her fingers through his hair, she arched her back while he sucked and pulled on her nipples with his lips. She moaned louder when he increased the suction.

Her voice was husky with desire. "I need you now."

Still wearing her lace g-string, she moved to the end of the bed on her knees, facing away from him. She spread her legs, and he got a full view of her tight ass and wet, puffy pussy lips behind the thin wisp of fabric. He admired how willing she was to expose herself.

"Such a good slut," he crooned admiringly, and when she giggled in response, her adorable laugh made him want to fuck her hard.

When Michael hadn't made a move after a few seconds, she looked over her shoulder at him and wiggled her ass. "Come fuck this dirty little slut."

Michael needed no other encouragement and he crawled over to her, grabbed the band of her g-string, and pulled it up so he could see it cut into her pussy. He contemplated removing it nicely, but was too impatient, so he ripped one of the thin strings holding it together. Alyssa gasped when she heard the material rip, but she didn't complain.

Starting at her toes, he caressed the arches of her feet and trailed his fingers up her leg just as he'd imagined earlier. When he got to her pussy, he gave it a stinging smack, and she jerked in surprise. He took a finger and traced the outside of her lips, the slippery moisture coating his finger. Her juice all over his finger was tempting to taste, but he was too impatient to wait any longer. He massaged her clit in soft circles with increasing strength. Alyssa moaned and pressed back against his hand. "Fuck me, now!" she gasped out and Michael knew he dared not wait any longer. Sitting up on his knees, he positioned himself against her ass and guided his cock towards her pussy.

"Now!" Alyssa moaned and attempted to move backwards to force him in.

Michael rubbed the tip of his cock against her wet slit and marveled at the silky smoothness of the lips guarding her entrance. Probing her hole but not going in fully elicited a groan from her that was almost a sob. Slowly pushing inside, he watched her pussy swallow his cock all the way to the base. The velvety soft folds of her skin encircled him like a glove as he nudged into her. Nothing in the world felt better than this moment. Pressed fully inside of her, he didn't move for a good half a minute, kneeling there, feeling her wonderfully tight pussy massaging the length of his rod.

Alyssa, getting impatient, started moving her ass in circles, forcing him to take action as well. He withdrew his cock totally from her so he could see it glisten with her juices, but moved back inside quickly when she gave a cry of protest. She bucked against him fast, so he knew she wanted it hard. He always wanted to please the woman he was with, so he gave her what she wanted.

He thrust into her fast, going deep with each push. She met him thrust for thrust, moaning. "Fuck me, fuck me harder." He hammered her pussy as she moaned out a variety of nasty things to him.

"I want to feel your enormous cock deep inside me."

"Make me come."

"Use me."

"Give me that magnificent cock."

"Fuck me harder than my husband!"

Her dirty talk and mention of a husband made him groan and spurred him to a greater sexual peak. He was getting close to coming, but wanted to make sure she got there first. Reaching his hand around her, he massaged her clit in circles. She squealed when his finger flicked faster, and began continually moaning, "Oh my god." She chanted her prayer to the sexual gods faster and faster until she bucked and shuddered underneath him, signaling her orgasm.

Only when he heard her breath catch and felt her body slowing down did he let himself finally come. He closed his eyes, grabbed her hips, and rocked against her roughly until he exploded. Her pussy milked his cock, and she shivered with aftershocks of pleasure while he shot several loads of his thick, sticky cum deep into her.

Having fully released his load, Michael paused, enjoying how he felt completely drained.

He pulled out of her and flopped backwards on the bed with a pillow under his head. She followed and snuggled against him. The scent of sex filled the air, and Michael loved how long the smell would linger in a room. They both were still breathing heavily and trying to catch their breath when Alyssa glanced over at him.

He smiled like a satisfied cat at her next words. "That was amazing."

Michael wiggled his eyebrows at her. "I know. I'm good."

She giggled at him. "I wish I really smoked. I would have one now."

He pulled her closer to him and she plastered against him, totally relaxed.

Alyssa cocked her head at him in question and poked him in the gut, asking, "Can you stay the night?"

Michael warred with himself. This hadn't been in the plan, but he wanted nothing more in the world to stay and forget his stressful week. When he pictured all the nasty, dirty things they would do all night long, he thought 'Fuck it.'

"Let me make a phone call to my house to see what's happening there."

He reached for the phone on the nightstand and dialed his home number. No one answered, and he punched in a zero when the voice machine came on so that he could check the messages. He relaxed as he heard his wife's voice tell him she ended up going to a friend's house and drinking too much, and that she was in no shape to drive so she was going to crash on the couch.

Michael smiled over at Alyssa. "You can have me all night long."

She grinned back at him. "I plan to."

In the morning, Michael groaned and rolled out of bed. Alyssa had kept him up all night with her multiple creative sexual positions. She continued to sleep while he showered and got dressed. He needed to leave, but went over to the bed and bent down to kiss her forehead. She stirred and cracked an eye open.

He smiled at her. "Morning, sleepyhead."

"Good morning," she mumbled groggily and rubbed her hands over her eyes. Seeing him fully dressed, she questioned, "You going so soon?"

"I need to get home and let the dog out."

She gave him a lazy smile and pulled him down by the shirt for one last kiss. "Ok, my love. I'll meet you at home after I shower and check out."

Michael beamed down at his wife. God, he loved this woman. Her voicemail on the machine last night almost made him break character. He never knew what to expect when she planned these roleplay nights. He strolled out of the hotel room with a swing in his step and felt energized.

As he climbed into his car that they had pre-arranged to be at the hotel already, he grinned like a fool. His wife was completely perfect for him. Life with her was never dull.

The End

FREEUSE FOR THE NIGHT

CHAPTER 1

"God, I'm so sore. I gave Ethan another free use weekend and let me tell you, he used me hard."

I freeze right before I turn the corner to walk into the break room to grab a cup of coffee. My coworker, Tanya, is speaking. She's a younger woman in her early 20s, super sweet and friendly.

A second woman remarks, "Shit, I wish I had a boyfriend. Your free use stories with Ethan always sound so hot. I really need to start dating again."

The second voice belongs to one of the newer hires, Fabiola. I had noticed Tanya and Fabiola eating lunch together and chatting during work hours since they hired Fabiola a month ago, so it doesn't surprise me they're close enough to share details about their personal lives.

Sex talk in the break room is a little risky, but I'm not one to judge since I've done it before. I'm approaching 40 though, so this was years ago when I was young and had a sex life to talk about. In the last year, things have gone extremely stale in the bedroom with my husband, Rich, so I have no juicy gossip to give out even if I had a work friend I'd tell.

Rich and I actually talked about it last Sunday after the third weekend in a row of no sex, and we're both taking the week to consider ways we can spice things up. The plan is to discuss our ideas Friday night and maybe get a little zing back for the weekend since the kids will be going camping with my brother and his family.

Sex has always been an important part of our marriage. We were high school sweethearts and everyone told us it wouldn't last, but we've made it 20 years now. We've had our trials like any couple, and usually the lulls in the bedroom had to do with our busy lives, especially when our two kids were younger. Now they're in their teens and more independent, so we could sneak off to our bedroom if we wanted, but the drive isn't there — at least not for him. Some days I'm so damn horny, I just want to rip his clothes off, but he's always tired or has a headache.

But what's free use? I'm afraid to enter the break room in case they stop talking when they see me. I'm hoping Tanya explains more, but when the topic turns to what color Fabiola should dye her hair next, I sigh and head in.

"Hi, Amanda!"

"Good morning, Amanda."

Both greet me and we chat while I fill my coffee mug and raid the pack of muffins that someone brought in to share. I select blueberry and my stomach grumbles, reminding me I skipped breakfast. I wish I had the guts to ask them what free use is, but I don't want them to know I was listening in. Once I have my coffee and muffin, I head out so they can go back to their private conversation.

When I get back to my desk, I'm still stumped about the conversation I overheard. Is free use some newfangled thing the younger generation is doing? If it was mainstream, I'm sure I would have heard about it by now. I'm tempted to search for it online, but hesitate.

I work in the office for a large trucking company and the owner is a loud, crass guy who has been in the industry for 40 years. An HR manager with strict demands for what should happen in a workplace to avoid lawsuits or law violations would not enjoy working here. Truckers are a more rough and rowdy crowd, so having a casual workplace is probably better.

I've also heard that the IT guy spends most of the day with his office door closed, jerking off and watching porn. I don't figure he'd take the time to check what I'm doing, but it's hard to shake the fear of being caught. But would it really matter if I searched for free use? As long as I avoid clicking on any video links and just look at the definition or articles, it should be fine... right?

Free use is a lot more mainstream than I realized. My search pulls up tons of articles and discussions about it. I'm fascinated as I click through the various explanations. The best ones are the detailed posts about what is consensual. From what I gather, I would give up control of my body to my husband and he would sexually use me however he wanted, though I'd have a safe word if things went bad. Another part of the kink is that sometimes the person being fucked doesn't respond to the sexual advances and ignores what is happening to them. *Hrm, could I even do that?*

It only takes me a moment to process. Yeah... shit, that's hot.

I try not to imagine it, but my mind goes to Tanya saying that her boyfriend, Ethan, used her hard all weekend. Tanya is attractive, and she has pictures of Ethan on her desk; he's fit and muscular. Now that I know what free use is, it's impossible to avoid visualizing what might have happened. It's been years since I've wanted to masturbate over someone at work, but my pussy clenches and the intense urge to rub myself while thinking about them fucking overwhelms me.

I struggle to imagine Rich doing whatever he wants to me, but I can't. He's not passive in the bedroom, but he's very focused on my pleasure. I doubt he'd be able to bend me over and take me with no consideration of my wants. A shiver runs down my spine and I press my pussy against my chair. God, I want it. This will be the thought I masturbate to when I'm alone, and I know just the toy to use. I recently bought a curved g-spot vibrating wand that always hits the perfect spot. I'll fuck myself with it and pretend it's Rich fucking me hard. Ugh, I really wish he was the type of guy who could do free use.

CHAPTER 2

For the next two days, all I can think about is having a free use night. Initially, I assumed the concept would be mostly for the guy's enjoyment, but my daydreams get filthier every day. Giving up control and being used like a sex toy is hot as fuck. I spend all day making decisions, and experiencing a night of pleasure where I do nothing but let someone else make all the plans and use me? Sign me up.

I know I wouldn't want to give up control all the time, but I can see the appeal of it occasionally. This will only work if Rich wants to fuck me multiple times in a day, and I'm not so sure of that anymore. I do light weightlifting twice a week in our tiny home gym tucked in the corner of our garage, plus I try to get in a daily 30-minute walk during lunchtime. I'm fit and attractive, so maybe this is just how it is after 20 years of marriage?

None of my friends have been married as long as I have, so it's difficult to gauge what is normal. Rich is great in bed when we do have sex, but the frequency is the issue. I've taken to masturbating whenever he's out of the house. It's cliche, but I really am like the horny housewife who notices all the hot dads in the neighborhood. I don't think I'd cheat on Rich. I'd ask to go to marriage counseling first, if it ever got to that point. It's just hard because I'm still incredibly sexually attracted to my husband, but he's slowing down as we age.

I can't get the free use idea out of my mind. I've been sneaking into the bathroom for two-minute breaks to rub myself furiously, and all I did was edge myself. It's driving me insane, and I need to find out if Rich has any interest at all.

On Thursday night, after being needy and wet all day, I decide to broach the subject with Rich at bedtime. If the thought is disgusting or he can't do it, I can use my time to come up with something else to suggest before we talk again tomorrow. We both sleep in the buff, so we're naked and pulling down the comforter and top sheet when I get the guts to ask.

"Hey hon? Have you ever heard of free use before?"

Rich pauses as he's fluffing his pillow. He gives me a wary glance. "Yes, why?"

I slide into bed and switch off the lamp on my nightstand, plunging the room into darkness. "Oh, no reason. It just sounds hot so thought we could try it."

Rich doesn't move for several seconds. Right when I'm about to ask him what's wrong, he climbs into bed and settles in on his back. He's quiet, and knowing my husband, I don't press him to talk. He's the type of guy who processes things slowly before he responds.

I adjust to the darkness and I can see faint outlines of everything. Eventually he turns onto his side, facing me with open eyes. We have a queen-sized bed, so I could easily reach out and caress his shoulders, chest, and stomach.

"Amanda, do you know what free use is?"

I smile, knowing he can't see. "Yes, love. It's when you use me however you wish."

"You'd want that?" His hand snakes across the bed and he twines his fingers in mine.

A deep yearning punches me in the gut and I don't know how to express my intense desire. I move his hand up to my mouth and kiss the back of it, letting my breath tickle his skin and simply say, "Yes."

Rich slides over and closes the distance between us, so I roll onto my side to face him. He embraces me and brushes his lips against mine before kissing me deeply, coaxing my mouth open for his tongue.

"Mmm." I moan against him and run my fingers along his neck and shoulder. Rich works out too, so his shoulders and arms are muscular. I love how strong he feels and I could watch him doing manual labor all day while his muscles ripple.

The longer the kiss lasts, the harder it is to concentrate on convincing him to try free use. I shift my legs slightly and feel moisture on my thighs while my pussy zings to life. I've been simmering all day, so it doesn't take much to get me going again.

When I move my hands across Rich's stomach, his muscles quiver and his stiff cock brushes my leg. *Oh, guess who woke up and joined the party.* I rub his shaft slowly for a moment and he groans against my lips before breaking off the kiss and grabbing my hand and removing my light grip on his cock.

I'm confused at what he's doing, but he presses me onto my back and uses one hand to pin both my wrists above my head, and moves the other between my legs. I spread open for him, and he chuckles a little as he slips his fingers between my slick folds.

"Oh, I think you really do like the idea of free use, don't you."

The way he words it is a statement and not a question. I'm too busy enjoying the spirals of pleasure running through my core to answer, so I stay silent. Fuck, I've missed this. It's been a long three weeks, and he rarely touches me at bedtime because he gets up early and needs his sleep.

"Amanda, look at me."

It's dark but I try to focus on his eyes since I can see the whites clearly.

"Hmm?" My head is spinning while he rubs circles on my clit.

Rich leans over and whispers in my ear. "Beg for it."

Oh, holy fuck. My brain blanks and I arch my back, trying to force his finger to rub rougher. His words put me in a frenzy and I'm desperate to come. I can't remember him ever telling me to beg before, though sometimes I do it on my own. Having him demand it is ten times more arousing.

I pant out, "Oh, my god," and moan. "Rich. Please, will you use me? PLEASE?"

He slips a finger inside me and presses in as far as he can reach, while he grinds his cock against my thigh.

"Hmm, I don't know. That wasn't good enough. Try again."

Jesus Christ. If I didn't want this so desperately, I might have told him to shove it, but instead I spew out all sorts of promises.

"Pretty, pretty, pretty please, will you please fuck me and use me all you want? I'll do anything for you. Anything you want. You can stick it anywhere, anytime, anyplace. I need it. I've been thinking about it for days. You can feel how wet I am. Please, Rich... please?"

I'm practically whimpering when I'm done begging and I'm not sure I've ever been this turned on in our entire marriage.

He withdraws his finger from my pussy and gives me a quick kiss while releasing my wrists.

"Yes, Amanda. Now get some sleep and we'll talk about this tomorrow night."

Um...

He rolls over, punches his pillow and snuggles in.

My body is on fire and I almost groan at being left wanting but hold it in. After all these frickin years of marriage, my husband just edged me? I don't know what got into Rich, but I'm still vibrating with need after he starts snoring gently. Fuck, if this wasn't so hot I'd slip out of bed and take care of things myself, but surprise – guess it looks like I enjoy being edged.

It's a long time before I finally fall asleep.

CHAPTER 3

Friday at work I'm so preoccupied with my free use fantasy that I keep making minor mistakes. Luckily nothing bad, and we have checks in place to catch the mistakes quickly, but I end up duplicating things and I'm unproductive. Rich is now the star of my daydream and remembering how turned on I was last night twists the mental image of my husband from a passive, jolly guy to someone who can take command.

Was he always like this, or did he just amp it up for my benefit since he loves to please me? A part of me feels that if he wanted to be more dominant in the bedroom, he would have done so already. But we were 15 when we started dating and who knows themselves at that age? It's possible he realized he wanted more control years later but didn't want to rock the boat.

I decide not to ask him. He's good at letting me know when he doesn't want to do something and from his response and how hard he was last night, he seems more than fine with the plan. We can talk about it afterwards and if it was just for me, next weekend we can explore a kink of his.

It's possible Rich has some secret fuck-the-maid fantasy that he's never disclosed. I could be down with wearing a little frilly skirt and nothing underneath. Just the thought of the maid outfit makes my panties wet and

I smile to myself. Yeah, maybe the maid idea is more for me, but I'm sure there has to be something he wants he hasn't told me about.

By the time my shift has ended, I'm a bundle of nervous energy. I keep wetting and biting my lips, and I have an odd fear that something is going to screw this up. My brother was scheduled to pick my kids up an hour ago, and I didn't get a text message about Uncle John being late, so I'm hoping that means they're gone. The camping trip getting canceled would fuck up the entire plan. We aren't doing free use tonight, and we're only going to talk about it, but I'm wet and aching for Rich to fuck me. He agreed to it, so I doubt he'll change his mind. He would have said he wanted to think about it if he wasn't sure.

The house is blissfully quiet when I get home and I shoot a text off to my sister-in-law asking if they got out of town on time. My brother usually drives, so I figured she would be the safer one to message. She replies that they are just leaving town now, and they got a later start than planned. I smile as I read since that's always the case. I've never been on a trip where I left on time.

I do a little happy dance around the kitchen once I know the trip is on. *Mama's getting laid this weekend!* I give a silent prayer to the gods that their car doesn't break down as I pour myself a glass of Merlot. I'm full of energy and it's hard to stand still. I'm sipping my wine and standing at the kitchen counter when Rich gets home.

Friday nights are takeout night and Rich picks up food after work. Tonight, he stopped at a local fish and chips place that also makes amazing clam chowder. The fish is okay, but we just want the chowder. He sets the bag on the counter and kisses the side of my neck, sending a shiver down my spine.

"I've been thinking about you all day, Amanda." The huskiness of his voice sends a rush through me and my pulse quickens. Wow, this free use thing has already spiced things up and we haven't even done it yet.

I give him a wide grin and a wink. "Oh, I've been thinking about you all day as well."

He pulls out soup bowls and splits the big styrofoam container of chowder into the bowls while I grab a beer from the fridge for him. When we sit down to eat, the soup is just as yummy as usual. We chatter about our day like normal, but my skin is sensitive to the slightest touch and I'm tingling. Every time he moves his hands, I imagine them caressing me. We're almost done eating before the topic finally turns. Rich is the first one to broach the subject.

"So, do you still want to try free use?"

I giggle before replying. "Yes."

"Did you have any thoughts on how you'd like it to work?"

Ooooh boy, I have tons of thoughts. "I was thinking maybe a free use Saturday, since the boys come home on Sunday?"

I don't want to sound demanding, but my pussy really wants him to use me whenever he wants tomorrow without me telling him what to do. He toys with his spoon while lost in thought.

"Um, but Rich?"

He focuses on me. "Yes?"

"I read that we should use a safe word in case I wish to stop."

"That's fine. What's your word?"

We already got to my safe word selection phase? Wow, he must really be serious about this.

I blush a little. "Lucy."

Lucy was another mom when my kids were in elementary school. Women never attracted me, but something about her made me hot to trot. I told Rich about the interest at the time and he loved to tease me about her and then fuck me, sometimes teasing me while we were fucking. Lucy and her husband moved across the country years ago and we didn't stay in contact, but Rich still likes to razz me about the one woman I would have been curious to sleep with.

Rich chuckles at me. "Perfect. So all day tomorrow?"

My pussy clenches and I try not to squirm. "Yes."

"From the time we wake until bedtime?"

I swallow. "Yes."

"And you'll do whatever I want whenever I ask?"

"Yes." I almost groan with my reply.

"It's a date."

My brain fogs with lust and I don't move when Rich stands up and starts clearing off the table. I'm still sitting there when he goes to leave the dining room and pauses.

"Oh by the way, nice begging last night."

That breaks me out of my stupor and I glance sharply at him. His eyes twinkle and he's got a wide, evil grin. If I'd had a pillow close by, I'd have thrown it at him. Instead, I just blow him a kiss. He chuckles as he heads into the kitchen.

I'm not sure how I'm going to make it through the rest of the night. My body thrums with need, and I can barely concentrate on the movie we watch after dinner. It was Rich's movie choice tonight, and he's forcing me to watch Star Wars: Episode IV - A New Hope for the umpteenth time. Our normal TV-watching position is Rich in the recliner section on the couch with me stretched out perpendicular to him with my feet in his lap. He loves the recliner, but I get the better deal because he usually gives me gentle foot and ankle rubs.

Since I've seen the movie before, it doesn't really matter if I daydream about tomorrow. I should have told him from dinnertime Friday night all the way through Saturday. Will I be able to sleep tonight?

My brain churns and I'm excited like a kid at Christmas, but his soft touch on my feet eventually lulls me and I calm down. By the time the movie's over, I'm yawning and I fall asleep before he does.

CHAPTER 4

A gentle tug on my nipple wakes me up the next morning. I'm groggy and wonder why he's pestering me so early. The fog clears quickly and a zing of lust makes me moan as his other hand joins in the fun and tweaks my other nipple. *Oh, fuck yes.* I'm instantly wet when I remember it's free use today.

Rich starts nibbling down my stomach and my breath catches when it looks like he might keep going, but he pauses at my navel.

"Amanda, last chance to back out. Do you want this?"

I moan out, "Fuck yes. Use me."

Rich grins and bites my belly gently. "Okay."

When he kisses his way back up towards my head, I give a tiny hiss of protest.

Rich laughs harshly as he spreads my legs and settles between them. "Did you think I was going to lick your pussy?"

Uh... I don't know how to answer him, so I stay silent.

"Remember today is MY free use of YOU."

He fits the head of his cock against my slick entrance, probing a little, and continues.

"You gave me a gift."

He presses in slowly as I moan at the exquisite pleasure of his rod burying itself all the way. He's slightly breathless, but goes on.

"So I'm going to come today as many times as I want without worrying about you."

Oh fuck, that's hot. I gasp as he drills into me leisurely, as if he's got all the time in the world — which I guess he does since I'm not going anywhere. I caress his shoulders and arms — anything I can reach, while I writhe underneath him. The pings of delight mount as he speeds up and I chant, "Oh, my god." as I spiral close to my orgasm.

Right before I come, Rich groans out and jerks inside me and blows his load.

"Ooooh, fuck," I groan out when I realize I'm not coming unless he finishes me with his hand or a toy.

Rich scoots off me, and I'm panting and dazed. I can't think clearly, but the realization that I might not orgasm today hits me like a semi-truck. *What did I sign up for?*

I want to come so badly. I'm breathing heavily, peeping out tiny sounds of distress, and close to actual tears when Rich spoons me.

He pulls me against him and kisses my shoulder. "Shhhh, calm down a little. I love you so much, Amanda."

He continues to give me soft kisses and whisper endearments as I come down from my sexual high. I've been so turned on for days, I never considered the fact I might not come. Actually, that's not correct. I considered it — I just didn't think he would fuck me and leave me hanging. This is a whole new side to my husband that I didn't know.

He continues to rub my back and side soothingly, and I eventually relax. Sighing, I melt into the bed. I'm still horny as all fuck, but it's not bad.

Rich's voice is soft. "You can change your mind at any point. If you don't want this, I don't either. Just say the word."

God, I love this man so much. Now that the frenzy has died down, everything seems better.

I flip around in his arms and kiss him deeply. "No, love. I want this."

He grins and pulls me against him tightly. "Good. Now let's get up and have some breakfast."

The next couple of hours are pretty mundane everyday Saturday stuff. We have waffles and eggs for breakfast, and he reminds me we need to go to the store today. I'm a little miffed that he wants to spend part of the day running errands. When I try to be cute and get him to go tomorrow, he shoots the idea down, saying he had too many things to do.

The crowded store puts me in a bad mood. Every minute we're out of the house is one less minute he might fuck me. I'm incredibly turned on still, and I want to grind against a hard surface, which is frowned on in public. When we get home and lug the groceries in, we fill all the kitchen counters. This is what it's like living with two teenagers.

Rich paws through the bags, putting away all the fridge and freezer items, which isn't typically what he does when we get home from the store. I'm confused as I work on his normal job, tucking the dry goods stuff away. We have a big walk-in pantry and when I unload what I carried in and turn the corner, he's by the door and I jump in fright.

"Jesus, you scared me!"

He grins and says, "Sorry," but doesn't look apologetic in the slightest. He follows me to the counter and I get an inkling of what is going on. My heart rate speeds up, and a gush of wetness leaks from me as he turns me towards the small kitchen table tucked in the corner.

I swallow a gasp as he pushes me over the surface and pulls my sweatpants and panties down to my knees in one swift movement. He fingers me and I try to ignore what he's doing as he rubs my clit and roughly plunges his digits into my pussy. I lose the battle when his cock replaces his hand and he rams his full length straight to my core.

"Oooh, fuck!" I groan as he repeatedly pounds into me. He's crazed and rougher than he's ever been. Each thrust knocks the table against the wall with a loud thud. The room spins as spikes of pleasure shoot from my pussy and I close my eyes, welcoming the building release.

It never happens.

Rich groans as he does one final sharp slam and deposits his second load for the day, bucking and rocking against me, coating my cave walls with his cum. He slumps against me for a moment, before withdrawing and pulling his shorts up. Opening my eyes, I stare blankly at the wall while my body vibrates with need — fuck.

Cum leaks out of me, and I don't move from the table for a few moments. Rich whistles a show tune and continues putting groceries away as if nothing happened. My senses are overwhelmed and I'm having a hard time collecting my thoughts. I'm not sure how much more of this I can take.

I finally gather my wits enough to stand up, and I do it slowly so I don't stumble. Pulling up my panties and sweatpants, I survey the kitchen and realize Rich finished with the groceries and is filling a glass at the sink. He comes and hands me the glass of water and kisses my forehead.

"Drink this."

I lift it to my lips mechanically and Rich watches to make sure I take a few sips. The water revives me a little and I'm feeling better, though still needy, and my pussy throbs. My heart rate slows down the more I sip, and I'm able to see the humor of the situation. *Did he have to take me this seriously with free use?*

In my fantasy, I was going to have three orgasms by midday. The anticipation of being used was misleading. I assumed I'd be ready to blow at the first touch, but Rich is doing a fabulous job of stopping right at the worst moment. What's funnier is that I don't think he's doing it on purpose. He's just doing what he wants and not planning on edging me.

"Amanda, are you doing okay?"

The worried tone of Rich's voice makes me focus on him. He looks genuinely concerned, and I give him a sheepish grin.

"Yes, love. I'm fine. Just catching my breath."

I wasn't lying. I really was fine. Today might not be going as I imagined it would, but it's still fucking awesome. It's been years since he's fucked me twice in one day, and I'm aroused and wet so the spice is definitely back. I just need to wrap my head around the thought that I might not come today. If I don't, he's so getting it tomorrow morning. I'll ride him and grind against him until I explode, even if he can't get hard. No need to tell him this though; I'll let it be a surprise if I don't get my orgasm tonight.

CHAPTER 5

Rich has some yard work he wants to do, so I do some light chores while I have the chance of keeping the house clean for more than 30 minutes with the kids gone. Obviously, I love my boys to death, but the concept of picking up after themselves without being reminded hasn't fully sunk in yet.

When I'm done with chores, I take a long shower and contemplate getting myself off with the shower head. Rich wouldn't know, and technically there's no rule saying I can't come without him today, but I'd still feel guilty. The anticipation of sex is keeping my pussy throbbing and if I got off, I'd relax and might not care as much about what Rich does. Not coming is a painful pleasure, and in small doses, it's obvious I like it — even though I hate it.

Just because I decide not to come doesn't mean I can't play with myself in the shower. I set the nozzle to pulsate and lean against the wall, propping a foot on the teak stool in the corner. Closing my eyes, I moan as the jets work their magic on my swollen bud. I gyrate my hips without moving my hand, so the force of the spray alternates between my clit and shooting against my cave entrance. I need Rich's cock deep inside me and I groan in frustration when I realize I'm making things worse for myself.

Turning the water off, I get out and dry off. I spend an extra moment rubbing the towel against my pussy and wonder when he's going to use me again. I'm hot and feverish, and not just from the shower. We always have a ceiling fan on in our bedroom because we need circulating air as we sleep, so I spread across the bed naked and let the soft breeze dry me completely.

I'm still tingling and tempted to play with my nipples and rub myself, but stop myself from doing it. I want to wait for Rich because I'm curious how the rest of the day will go. Knowing I could use my safe word at any point is reassuring, but I wanted this and I'm determined to see it through. The fun of introducing a new aspect of play into our marriage is worth potentially being frustrated all day. But Rich really wouldn't do that to me, would he?

This new side of Rich makes everything uncertain. I don't know if this Rich would make sure I come. He's clearly having a grand ole time, though I appreciate that he's checking on me afterwards. I sigh and drag myself off the bed, pulling on shorts and a tank top. I get a slutty thrill when I opt to not put on clean panties and go commando.

Rich is still doing yard work, so I relax on the couch and read a smutty short story on my tablet while I wait. I search for a new book to download and focus on the free use erotica genre. I'm halfway through a book titled "Free Use Friday," when I set it aside because I'm getting too worked up.

My situation differs greatly from the book, but I kept picturing myself as the woman in the story and imagining what my husband would do if one of his friends came over every Friday and used me. No way in hell would Rich be as accommodating as the husband in the story, and that's perfectly fine. I enjoy how Rich occasionally gets jealous if he thinks other men are flirting with me. It's stupid, but it gives me warm fuzzies to know he loves me enough that he doesn't want to share.

When Rich comes inside, he takes a shower and we eat a salad for dinner — neither of us wanted to eat anything too heavy. I'm still turned on and my skin is extra sensitive. Whenever I brush against something, I shiver.

Rich is being liberal with his caresses and kisses today. While we were making the salad, I noticed he was hard, but he did nothing about it.

When I realize I'm biting my lip and disappointed that he didn't use me while we were fixing dinner, I giggle at the thought. *Yeah, I'm hopeless and just want his cock.* I'm not usually this cock-hungry, but this week has been rough and it's sex on my mind, all the time.

CHAPTER 6

After dinner, he suggests we watch a show, but this time he doesn't use the recliner. He sits at one end of the couch and pulls me onto his lap. I'm not expecting this and gasp when he pulls me down on top of him, but I quickly warm up to the idea and settle in, wiggling my ass against his cock with the pretense of getting comfortable. I get a zing of satisfaction as I feel him stiffen underneath me — *take that!*

Rich chooses an unsolved true crime episode and I'm immediately drawn into the drama of a bank robbery in the late 1800s. Halfway through, Rich spreads my legs and slips his hand down my shorts and into my panties. We're both facing the television and he can't see my face, so I smirk and keep watching. *Oh, this is how it's going to be, is it?*

I'm determined to ignore him this time, but when his finger brushes my clit and slides into my pussy to gather some moisture, I almost moan. *Okay, fuck... I need to concentrate or he'll have me begging soon.* I don't want to give him the satisfaction of knowing how much he's affecting me today, or how desperate I am to come.

He continues to make soft circles around my hard bean, and it's impossible to pay attention to the show. I keep my eyes trained on it, but let my mind wander and enjoy the pleasure radiating from my core. It's all I can do to not grind against his hand as he slips two digits into my pussy and finger fucks me for a moment.

We're both silent, and he picks up the intensity of his rubbing. He stops long enough to force me to lift up so he can pull my shorts off, and then spreads my legs wide open so he has complete access to my honey pot. When he goes back to what he was doing, I realize I've totally lost the plot to the show.

I almost lose it when Rich holds all his fingers together and uses the flat side of his fingertips to brush my clit furiously back and forth. My pussy involuntarily clenches, and a spurt of wetness runs down my crack. My leg muscles twitch and it's all I can do to not cry out and buck against his hand.

I hide a sigh of relief when he stops rubbing me, but it's only a temporary reprieve because he forces me onto my back on the couch next to him and spreads my legs again. I bite my bottom lip and close my eyes when he attacks my pussy with his mouth. *Oh, holy fuck.*

Rich pulls my outer lips open with his thumbs, uses the flat portion of his tongue to lick along my entire crease, and then focuses on my clit. My hips give a tiny jerk and I hope he doesn't notice while I tense all my muscles to hold myself still. The room is spinning even with my eyes closed, and I can't think of anything except his magical mouth as energy shoots through my body.

When he plunges two fingers into my cave and finger fucks me while continuing to suck on my clit, I'm lost.

"Oooh, my god!"

Moaning out, I reach down and press his head against me so I can grind my pussy up against his face. Rich welcomes the roughness and licks for all he's worth, sucking and swirling his tongue around my clit. I thrash around as waves of pleasure wash over me. My stomach muscles quiver and my thighs tense, and I'm going to come any moment.

"Oh god, Rich. Don't stop."

Of course, my asshole husband stops.

I mewl in distress, and he sits up and slaps my pussy, making me jerk and cry out.

"Get up. We're moving to the bedroom."

I struggle to sit up, and he has to help me. Dazed, I can't think of anything except doing whatever it takes to orgasm. I leave my shorts behind and dutifully follow him, stripping off my tank top as soon as we enter the room. He leaves the light off and pushes me onto the bed on my back.

His voice is thick and rough. "Move up to the pillow."

I do what he says, and he strips out of his clothes and climbs on top of me. My heart pounds and I shiver from desire. I open my legs so he can nestle between them, and my clit throbs as he brushes the head of his cock against it.

"Rich, oh my god, fuck me!"

I try to arch up against him, and he laughs as he rubs up and down my slit.

"Is this what you want?"

"God, yes."

Rich preses just the tip inside my pussy and then pulls out and gently taps his cock against my clit.

"You sure? I don't know if you want it enough."

I moan and whine. "Please? Oh god, please Rich?"

When he finally thrusts all the way inside me, I groan "God, yes" and strain against him, but the relief is short-lived. He withdraws again and pats the tip against my swollen bean.

Rich commands, "I want you to beg, now that I know you do it so well."

Oh, fuck.

"I can't think. Please don't make me beg." I'm whimpering and almost close to tears. I need to come so badly, why won't he just fuck me?

"Amanda?"

My voice is tiny and sad, and I just want him to put me out of my misery. "Yes?"

He switches to a soothing tone. "Amanda honey, look at me."

My head is spinning and my vision is blurry, but I try to focus on him.

"I love you so much, and I'll fuck you and you're going to come so hard. But you have to beg for it. Okay?"

Ooooh. When he says I'll come, my pussy clenches and my nipples harden. I arch against him, desperate, but resolved to beg better than I did the other night. Anything to get me an orgasm faster.

I gasp out in a rush anything I can think of that he's ever asked for. "Oh, god Rich. Please fuck me. Fuck me harder than you've ever done before. Use me however you want. Just please, please, PLEASE let me come. Pretty please? I'll do anything for you, I'll do your laundry for a week, I'll massage your feet, anything — please let me come. I'll wear the slutty nun outfit you joked about. I'll give you a striptease, I'll fully shave, I'll go to baseball games with you. Just oh my god, PLEASE let me come. PLEASE fuck me."

I'm panting when I finish. He doesn't answer, but plunges his cock straight to my core. I scream out, "Oooh, fuck yes!" as delight ripples through me.

Rich destroys my pussy. He fucks me furiously, banging against me hard with each forward thrust. I quiver as my entire body heats and energy builds deep inside. I'm edging closer to the summit as he hammers me relentlessly.

I moan and chant, "Oh my god," and the surge of bliss overtakes me. I squeal as I peak, convulsing and milking his cock as my cave walls shudder around him. The orgasm seems as if it lasts forever as I buck and tremble and my mind goes blank.

I experience a moment of pure rapture as a second surge overwhelms me and I climax again. I scream out nonsense as I ride the double wave and writhe against him. Rich groans loudly and he halts all movement, while his body spasms and he spurts load after load of his hot seed deep inside my pussy. He pumps into me a few more times before collapsing on top of me.

We both lie there, panting and spent, for a long time. *Holy fuck, that might have been the best sex of our marriage.* Rich finally climbs off and snuggles by my side. We've both sticky with sweat and the room smells like sex, but I don't want him to move away. I need the comfort of him against me.

Rich kisses my shoulder. "I love you so much, Amanda."

"Mmmm." I still can't form words, but I find his hand and entwine his fingers with mine, giving them a light squeeze.

We're silent for a while longer, both coming down from the rush, and when my heart rate slows, the fuzziness in my brain finally clears enough for me to talk.

"I love you too, Rich."

He moves down and pillows his head against my breast, and I wrap my arm around him.

He's hesitant when he asks, "Would you want to do that again?"

I pause for a moment, but know that everything that happened today turned me on more than I've ever been.

I chuckle a little when I answer. "Yes, but maybe only for special occasions."

Rich hums and sounds happy. "Deal."

I stroke his back, almost drifting to sleep, when he speaks again.

"I think we need a nun costume."

I smile in the darkness, remembering what I offered while I begged. *Shit, I guess I better get online and start shopping.*

The End

Nurse for the Night

CHAPTER 1

"Josie, I want you to wear a nurse costume."

It's a normal Monday night and my husband, Dan, and I are curled up on the couch snuggling and watching a medical drama TV show when he springs his request during a commercial break. Halloween was only a couple of weeks ago and he tried to get me to dress up with him as a doctor and me as a nurse. I already had plans on being Flo from Progressive Insurance so I turned him down, but I couldn't help joking with him that he's sexist and maybe I wanted to be the doctor. I'm a little confused at what he's talking about. Why is he bringing it up again?

"It's a little early for next year's Halloween planning. Don't you think?"

I'm only half listening to him because the TV is playing a commercial about refinancing your mortgage and I'd been wondering if we should do that. It's probably a bad idea, right?

"I mean in the bedroom. Not Halloween."

Okay, that got my attention.

"What?"

I try to keep my voice modulated so I don't sound like I'm kink-shaming my husband. We have 17-year-old twins, Kara and Melissa, who attend a liberal public high school and I've learned to be open-minded with whatever's thrown at me. Let's just say Kara leads a very interesting life, and more power to her. If I was her age, I'd probably be doing similar things since I was a bit unruly before I met Dan. He and I hooked up our senior year and got married right out of high school because I was pregnant with the twins. That left little time to go too crazy, and he never asked me to wear a nurse outfit in all these years.

Whenever we're watching TV together, he's usually sitting at one end of the couch while I'm tucked under his arm with my legs stretched out the length of the cushions. I've got long, red, curly hair and he likes to play with the curls as we snuggle. Since it's almost winter, I'm wearing sweats, fuzzy socks, and still considering finding a blanket on the next commercial break. Sexy time is the furthest thing from my mind.

He didn't say anything after I asked him 'what,' so I swing my feet to the floor so I can sit up straight and see his face. I contemplate him, waiting for him to speak.

"Don't look at me that way. Nurses are sexy!"

Since I purposely kept my expression neutral, I figure it's his own shame over this naughty fantasy that has him reading something that isn't there. I'm mainly curious how long he's been thinking about this before he asked me last month. His Halloween request seems suspect now. He should have been open about what he wanted in the first place when he suggested the costumes, and I bet I would have been down for it. We'd had several adult drinks Halloween night and I was in a VERY friendly mood.

I don't know what someone does as a nurse in the bedroom, but I'm willing to try. How hard can it be? Besides, a couple of months ago, he wore a pair of faded jeans and his old cowboy boots and hat, and let me ride him. It's only fair I play along with this kinky request.

I give him my best sassy grin. "Okay, let's do it."

Dan lets out a whoosh of air and his body relaxes, as if he was getting ready to do battle before I answered. I snuggle back into his side and we're both silent as we finish the show. My mind whirls trying to figure out how to make this fancy of his work. The internet better have good information or else I'm fucked — or not fucked if he's turned off by what I do.

CHAPTER 2

My work schedule starts earlier than Dan's, so I'm always home a couple of hours before him. I use my alone time that Tuesday to hunt for a nurse outfit and I'm surprised at the variety of options the biggest online shopping website offers. So many choices, that can all be delivered to me by Thursday — who would have thought?

I order a set that comes with a short white lab coat, a fake stethoscope, a nurse hat, white fishnet thigh-high stockings, and a pair of plastic gloves. The gloves give me pause and I consider why I would need them. Hopefully, they are just for looks and he's not expecting me to do anything too... uh... invasive... I probably should discuss this more with him before we do it, but if I'm the nurse, I'm the one in charge, so he's going to just accept whatever ministration I feel like giving him.

I giggle when I get a slight sexual thrill from thinking about Dan lying in bed while I "tend" to his "needs." Fuck, this is going to be hilarious. How will I keep a straight face? Maybe I can be a jolly nurse who cracks jokes. Not all nurses have to be serious. I could give myself a silly name to go with my character, like Nurse Badonkadonk or Peaches because Dan loves my ass. Yeah, Nurse Peaches is good. There is no way I'd be able to keep a straight face and call myself Nurse Badonkadonk.

Since the outfit will be delivered on Thursday, I pull up my household's joint calendar on my phone to see what the family has going on in the upcoming weeks. I need to find a night that Kara and Melissa are out of the house for a long stretch of time. No one wants to walk in on mommy dressed up as a nurse while servicing daddy.

Once the girls got old enough and we trusted them with smartphones, I signed up for a shared calendar app and it's gone surprisingly well. Everyone updates their schedule with what is going on, and the girls have learned that if they don't put it on the calendar so that I can see it, there's no guarantee of a ride to their event. Someday they might take driver's training, but they seem to lack motivation and it hasn't happened yet, so Dan and I still get to play chauffeur.

When I realize that Melissa already blocked off this Saturday as the day she's out of town with her youth group to help clean and fix up an elderly lady's home, and then they're all having a slumber party at the church afterwards, excitement shoots down my spine. Oh fuck, this might happen sooner than I thought. I just need to ship Kara off, and then the entire night is ours.

Kara is at her girlfriend's house right now — supposedly — so I send her a quick text message.

`Can you find somewhere else to be Saturday evening and all night?`

It doesn't take long for her to reply.

`Why?`

Of course, I'd birth a kid who asks questions when I tell her to get lost. Melissa would say yes so fast my head would spin, all tickled about the opportunity to do something out of the house. But Melissa has a large group of friends and is extremely outgoing, while Kara has only a couple of close friends she likes to bring to our house instead of staying at theirs.

But Kara and I also have very open communication about sex — much more so than I do with Melissa — so I have no problem teasing Kara a little.

Because I want to have a wild night with your father, and I don't want you home.

I snicker as I wait for her reply, and she doesn't disappoint me.

`Ewwww gross. Consider me gone.`

Satisfied that I've cleared the house for Saturday, I open an internet browser to search for naughty nurse roleplay ideas. I don't even get a chance to click on a link before my phone dings that someone added an event to the calendar. I glance at the notification and see that Kara is staying the entire night at her girlfriend's house.

Part of me wars with being okay with her staying with her significant other, but I also know how I was at that age. It doesn't matter whether you're spending the night, things are going to happen. I'd rather she be safe and honest about where she is than make her sneak around and hide stuff. Dan doesn't want to think about it or talk about it, so the girls both come to me about their boyfriends and girlfriends. He'd prefer to pretend that they're still 10 years old, but I was dating Dan at 17, so deep down he knows what's up.

I push aside my worry about the twins and focus on my immediate concern — finding out how to be a sexy nurse. Within minutes, I'm lost on the internet, and an hour blinks past. When Dan pops into the computer room to find out what I want to do for dinner, I'm startled that he's home already. Shit, where did the time go?

But my online search didn't let me down and I'm armed with a plan. My man is getting a general checkup on Saturday.

CHAPTER 3

When the nurse costume arrives on Thursday as scheduled, I shove it in the back of our bedroom closet without opening it. I'm curious what it looks like, but I want to wait until the kids leave on Saturday, so I hold off on digging in. If something is wrong with it, I'll improvise with some yellow kitchen gloves, a wooden spoon, and a forehead thermometer. I'll tell him the hospital has budget cuts and this is now the quality of service he can expect. Once my hands are on his cock, he won't care and he'll still give the ward an A+ rating when I'm done with him. But hopefully it doesn't come down to that.

Dan and I talk briefly later that night about expectations, and he's down for whatever I want to do. He claims he'll be the best patient ever and take all his prescribed medication. Part of me hoped to play bad nurse and force him to do what I say, but it's his fantasy and if he wants caring and supportive, I'll go with it. That doesn't stop me from daydreaming and getting wet thinking about corralling a disobedient patient and punishing him. The more I think about this roleplay scenario, the more eager I get. Why isn't it Saturday already?

Kara is the last to leave on Saturday. She gives me a mock disgusted look when I blow her kisses and tell her not to have as much fun tonight as I'm going to have. I get too much joy from teasing Kara. She and I have talked in the past, and she told me she knows her father and I have sex, so as long as I don't give her details there's no need to pretend it's not happening. I was the same way at her age, and it always amused me when my friends were disgusted at the thought of their parents having sex. Melissa is more like Dan and wants to believe everyone in the house is a virgin. I leave her be with her visions of immaculate conception.

As soon as the front door closes behind Kara, I scurry to our closet and pull out the package. Dan is under strict orders to stay in his basement "game room" until I text him to come upstairs. I hope he's downstairs stroking and thinking about tonight. I'm still not totally sure what to do, but anticipation has kept me wet all day. My pussy is ready for some action.

I put the box on my bed, and I examine each item for defects as I pull them out. Everything appears to be fine, thank God. Looks like human resources staffed the hospital tonight and all services are a go!

I've been debating all week what to wear under the short white lab coat and I finally settled on a black lace negligee. I slip it on, opting for no panties, and put my foot up on the bed to pull up the white fishnet thigh-high stockings. Admiring myself in the full-length mirror behind the door, a tiny bolt of pleasure pulses from my pussy. Dang, I'm hot. I really should dress up in sexy lingerie more often. So far, this seems more for me than for Dan. I'm dripping wet from making the plans and the ritual of dressing the part. Maybe I should have worn panties after all? Nah, it'll be fine.

At thirty-seven, I'm not ready to be put out to pasture yet, but it's easy to let yourself go after so many years with the same person. Sure, I've got a softer stomach than I'd like, but my ass is still high and firm — which pleases Dan to no end since he's an ass man. But for most people, it's my naturally red curly hair and my breasts that draw the attention. My tits aren't so huge that they give me a backache or I need reduction surgery, but they are more than generous. In a push-up bra, I look pretty amazing and I wear deep V-neck shirts to emphasize my cleavage when I dress up. I might as well work with the "gifts" the universe gave me, and the sly glances I get from other men and women boost my ego.

I stop admiring myself, slip on the lab coat, and place the stethoscope around the back of my neck with the ends dangling down the front of the jacket. Picking up the nurse hat, I try it out and critique myself in the mirror. No matter how I arrange it, I look campy. Yeah, this won't work. Nurse Peaches works in a high-class hospital, so I ditch the hat. There, now I seem like a skilled nurse. I giggle to myself as I glance down at my fishnet stocking-covered feet and no shoes. Yes, totally professional here. Nurse Peaches is on the job!

I clean up the discarded packaging, lay the plastic gloves on the nightstand, and drape my husband's terrycloth robe on the end of the bed. It's time to notify my patient that his room is ready.

When I leave the bedroom, I tiptoe to the computer room, glancing around for my husband in case he disobeyed my order and is upstairs. I don't want him to see me until he's in bed and lying down. Looks like Dan is a good boy and I close the door to the computer room and sit down in my office chair before I text him.

Sir, this is Nurse Peaches. Your private room is ready for you. Please go to it and strip. There is a bathrobe on the bed. Put it on and lie down on your back. I'll be with you in ten minutes exactly.

I add an emoji smiley face at the end. We're a friendly hospital and like to give a more "personal touch" whenever possible. Dan replies quickly.

Yes, ma'am. I'm omw. I appreciate all your help.

I debate about the ma'am bit. I guess Nurse Peaches wouldn't mind being called ma'am so I'll allow him to continue using it if he wants to.

The ten minutes take an eternity and I have to remind myself to breathe while I wait. I'm getting worked up and I haven't even seen the patient yet. To amuse and distract myself, I spin circles in my office chair and check my phone every couple of minutes. After six minutes, my honey pot throbs from anticipation and I can't take it any longer. Stopping the momentum of the chair, I spread my knees and slip my hand up and under my nightie, fingering my wet pussy and using the lubrication to caress my swollen clit. I lean back and get lost in the moment, sighing as tendrils of pleasure blossom from my core. When a moan slips out, I'm shocked out of my sexual daze. Oh fuck, how long has it been?

CHAPTER 4

I stroll into the room with an efficient mien and smile at Dan.

"Hello, sir. I'm Nurse Peaches and I'm here to service you tonight."

Oh, fuck. I sound stupid. My opening line sounded better in my head. I should have written a script and practiced.

Dan flashes me a goofy grin, seeming not to care, and answers in a stilted, exaggerated tone. "Thank you for fitting me into your busy schedule. I'm hot and ache all over. I don't know what is wrong with me. Can you help me?"

I almost bust out laughing. Shit, this is hilarious. He's obviously been thinking of a script in his head as well. Luckily, I'm able to keep my professional demeanor.

"Oh? I'll give you a VERY thorough examination. We'll find out what's wrong with you."

I approach the side of the bed and undo the belt tie on his robe. When I push it open at the chest, he's naked underneath as requested, and I'm overwhelmed with the desire to break from my role, hop on top of him, and grind away. At least, that's what my wet and needy pussy wants, but we may never do the naughty nurse roleplay again, so I want to give him a decent experience.

I slide the earpieces of the stethoscope in place and press the flat round end against his chest. I purposely brush my fingers along his skin while I'm pretending to listen. He shivers slightly but I'm not sure if it's from the cold stethoscope or from my fingers.

"Give me two deep breaths."

His chest expands and contracts while I glance down towards his cock. The robe didn't open all the way, but I can see a growing bulge underneath the terrycloth. I lick my lips and imagine his cock in my mouth. That will definitely be part of my nursing duty.

"I'm going to just palpate around a little. Tell me if anything is tender."

"Yes, ma'am."

Dan's voice is hoarse when he answers, and the corners of my mouth twitch while I try to hold back a smile. If I make it through to the end of tonight without laughing my ass off, it's going to be a miracle.

I lay the stethoscope on the nightstand, bend over him and start at his head. My boobs are practically in his face as I massage his scalp a moment, before tickling his earlobes and rubbing the lobe of each ear between my index finger and thumb. His ears are an erogenous zone for him and I have to hold back from bending down even closer and sucking on one. I lightly trace my fingers down the sides of his neck and push open the robe even further as I focus on his chest.

Dan's breathing heavily, as I skim my fingernails through his thin patch of chest hair. He's never been able to grow a beard, but he's finally got some chest hair, after it's taken years to fill in. He likes to joke that at 35, he started growing hair in weird places, including his chest, and it might sound funny but it's true. Before then, I had his four chest hairs named. George was the longest and my favorite, but now I can't even find George because there are too many of them.

Not being able to help myself, I lean close and press my lips to his nipple, flicking the tiny bud with my tongue while my hands search lower, inching ever so slowly towards his cock. My patient is being such a good boy and keeping still and quiet, so I want to reward him.

I push open the robe and his cock is at full attention, ready to be examined. I nibble and kiss down the length of his chest and he tenses as I approach his groin with my mouth. Caressing the underside of the head of his cock with my fingers, I gently lick the tip. Dan inhales sharply and my pussy responds with a corresponding throb.

Purring at him, I attempt to sound as sexy as possible. "Is this spot causing you any trouble?"

When I swirl my tongue around the head, Dan groans and responds, "Yessss, that's the spot that hurts. I think it needs a massage or something."

I dip my head so he can't see my stupid grin, while I rub my palm down the full length of his shaft and fondle his balls. When I move down the shaft with a series of gentle kisses and grip his balls tighter, he arches his back and moans. "Oooh, that feels good."

Uh-oh, looks like Dan broke character. I stop kissing on him, but keep playing with his balls. "We aren't here for pleasure. I'm trying to find out what's wrong with you. Now cough for me."

Dan swears softly under his breath and I hear an, "Oh fuck," before he pretend coughs while I tug on the family jewels. His cock sways and a bead of precum leaks out.

I take on a concerned tone and tell him, "Oh, I see what the problem is now."

"Oh?" He's breathless and has a pained expression on his face.

"Yes, look at this."

I grip the base of his cock and give it a firm yank.

"Wha..." Dan isn't able to form a complete word and his cock spasms, while he gives a strangled moan and looks down at what I'm doing.

"You're all swollen here. This must be really frustrating you, you poor thing." I give him my best sympathetic smile. "Don't worry, Nurse Peaches will fix you right up. I know just the thing you need."

I really don't know what the fuck I'm doing, but Dan seems to love all of it. If I'd been recording this, I'd have cringed and stopped it after five minutes, but the pretend aspect of the scenario turns me on more than I imagined it would. My only dilemma is if I suck him off and he comes, then I don't get his glorious cock in my pussy. I mean, if I were an excellent nurse, I'd do what's best for the patient, right? But maybe I'm not that good.

He's leaking more precum, and I decide to put him out of his misery part of the way by gently flicking the underside of the tip with my tongue. I take my time with it, licking back and forth, and up and down, before slipping my lips over the entire tip and swirling my tongue against him before pulling away again. I tease him by doing this a couple of times, and he's pumping his hips slightly, trying to shove more of his cock into my mouth. But that's not going to happen here. I'm the one in control here and I've decided I want his cock buried deep inside me.

Straightening up, I put on my professional voice again. "Okay, I need you to roll onto your stomach. It's time to check out your backside."

Dan's lust glazed eyes search out mine, and he's confused. "What?"

"You heard me. Roll over."

He's hesitant when he agrees. "Uh, okay."

While he rolls over, taking care to position his stiff cock in a comfortable position, I pick up the plastic gloves from the nightstand and silently slip them on. He's too distracted to notice what I'm doing. Once he's settled onto his stomach, I untangle the robe out from around his body, helping him get his arms out of the sleeves, and I toss it on the floor. That's when he notices the gloves.

He's alarmed. "Wait, what are those for?"

I turn my head so he can't see my face and I stifle my giggle. Oh fuck, he thinks he's about to get anally probed. He and I have talked about trying that, so it's a reasonable assumption on his part, but that isn't my plan.

I swing my hand back and bring it down hard and swift on an ass cheek with a loud smack.

"Hey!" Dan jerks his legs and his toes wiggle. "How does this help me feel better?"

Instead of answering, I give his other cheek a firm whack.

Dan shifts and looks like he's almost purposely humping the bed. He grumbles, "What sort of hospital is this?"

I don't like the gloves and want to feel his warm skin, so I pull them off. I toss them on the floor and climb up on the bed on my knees next to him. When I massage his ass checks with my hands, he relaxes and sighs.

"Oh, yes. That's better."

A giggle escapes, and I clamp a hand over my mouth and compose myself before removing it.

"I was only checking your reflexes. Everything seems fine."

I continue to rub his ass with one hand while brushing the other hand up the length of his back, prodding and massaging his spine. I hit a sensitive spot and Dan shivers.

My pussy is a wet mess and I really can't do much more of this. He and I didn't discuss a timeline of how long I was going to play nurse, but this nurse needs to come.

"I'm almost done with my evaluation, sir, and I think if we relieve the pressure of your swollen body part, you'll feel all better."

Dan mumbles an, "Oh, yes," into the pillow, but I'm still able to understand him.

"Okay, then roll over again."

He wastes no time flipping onto his back, and since I'm on the bed too he moves towards the center to give us both room. Once he settles in, his engorged cock practically pulsates at me. Ooooh, yes, that's what I need. But first, I pause and pick up one of his hands, moving it down to his cock. I'm still on my knees next to him and I slip a hand between my thighs and finger my pussy.

My voice is husky when I command, "Stroke yourself nice and slow. I want to watch."

"Oh, god," he groans out, but does what I say.

"Mmmm, nice," I moan at him as I caress circles around my swollen bean. We're both breathing heavily, and I speed up my hand and my thighs quiver. He's still moving his hand slowly, but I want to drive him towards the edge.

I'm panting and harsh when I tell him, "Beat your dick for me."

He moans out a "Yes," and immediately speeds up, pulling on his cock harder than I would have.

"Fuuuuck, I'm going to come."

Oh, hell no, he's not.

"Stop!" I bark out.

Dan whimpers and moves his hand away.

Knowing that he's going to blow his load really fast once he's inside me, I continue to work my clit.

"I want you to lie there and watch me for a minute."

I shift on the bed, getting on my hands and knees, and pull up the lab coat and nightie so that my bare ass is facing him. I lean my chest toward the bed so I'm resting on one forearm and slip the other hand underneath me to play with my pussy and clit.

Fingering myself without restraint, I alternate between stroking as deep inside as I can reach and flicking my bean in a perfect rhythm that drives me towards the edge. I continue for a few moments as heat builds at my center. Spikes of pleasure ping my brain as I speed up my rubbing, and for one brief second I consider making him watch me orgasm. But I really want to come all over his cock, so I stop when my thighs tense and I think I'm about to come.

Ugh, fuck. I need it in me, NOW! I turn around to face Dan and climb on top of him. He's been watching me like a good boy the entire time and almost looks blissed out as I guide his cock to my entrance and press down. I stretch and mold around him and squeal in pleasure when I give an experimental pump of my hips.

I bring his hands to my waist so he can grip me as I bounce on him, grinding against him with each downward motion.

"Ohhh, Josie. Fuuuuck!"

I'm too far gone to care that he broke character as I spiral towards release. I close my eyes and focus on the intense sensations every time I drive down hard and force him in as deep as he can go.

Dan cries out, "I'm coming!" as he jerks and spasms underneath me.

My orgasm rips through me when I feel his cock twitch and the spurt of his warm cum. I shudder and writhe as ecstasy radiates all the way to my toes and fingers. I don't slow down and continue to ride him, trying to milk every drop out of him I can get, as waves of delight wash over me.

When Dan softens inside me, I slow down and open my eyes. He's got a pained expression on his face, so I quickly climb off him and he relaxes. Ooops, didn't mean to ride him until he was too sensitive. I obviously AM a bad nurse.

I'm hot and sweaty, so I pull off the lab coat and toss it towards the end of the bed before collapsing and snuggling against his side. Being this close to him is still too warm for me, but I need the closeness as we both calm down.

I'm drifting, satisfied and a little proud of myself for pulling that off, when Dan breaks the silence.

"Nurse Peaches?"

I giggle and don't try to hide it this time. "Yes?"

Dan's voice is sleepy, and he's obviously ready to zonk out. "I feel so much better now. Thank you."

I kiss the side of his chest and cuddle closer to him. "You're welcome."

His breathing evens out and I think he's asleep, so I'm surprised when he mumbles, "Gonna give you a ten star rating."

I smile as I close my eyes, knowing I'll have to get up soon, but a cat nap sounds perfect and I deserve it. After all, I just gave ten star service.

The End

USED FOR THE NIGHT

Chapter 1

My eyes widen as my husband fills the crystal candy bowl full of green and red condoms and sets it on the sturdy wooden coffee table in the rec room. He must have dumped 50 condoms in the bowl, creating a festive holiday look among the Christmas themed pillows, Santa doll collection, and the tree.

"Uh... Jon... I thought you only invited 20 guys?"

Jon arranges them so the tiny foil packets are laying flat and glances towards me with a twinkle in his eye and his adorable, goofy smirk.

"Only 20 are coming, but maybe someone will want two."

My breath catches as a gush of wetness hits my panties at his words. Shit, this is so fucking hot. I can't believe Jon agreed to this.

Two years ago, Jon and I opened our marriage, and I started sleeping with my bosses in a hotwife arrangement. This lead to me also being a birthday gift to various people. For a while, it was a blast, and Jon had no desire to sleep around. He just wanted to screw me after I got home while I told him all the dirty details and we recreated some of the sexy parts.

It was pretty fabulous for over a year, but once Jon realized he was into BDSM, my eagerness to fuck other guys lessened and I stopped sleeping with my bosses. We never officially said we were stopping the hotwife thing, and the door is still open to the possibility. I just haven't felt the need in a long time. These last couple of years revitalized our sex life, and I love Jon more than ever.

Since we both became more candid about our sexual needs, about three months ago I confessed to Jon that I had a secret yearning to wear a blindfold and be used by a bunch of men at a party. As soon as I told him my sluttiest fantasy, he turned into a beast and fucked me so hard I saw stars. That night is in my top five favorite sex experiences and whenever I recall it, I shiver in delight. Jon in beast mode is spectacular to behold.

We've been talking the fantasy off and on since then, and every time we discussed how it would work, it ended up with him fucking me from behind while making me beg to be used. My fantasy quickly turned into something he got off to, and we had many fun nights roleplaying the idea.

Which leads us to today, this holiday party. With it being the holiday season, it was easy enough to turn it into a Christmas party, and it's been a running joke with Jon that it's my Christmas gift. Santa's coming early for me this year — hopefully coming more than once.

I've been a horny mess, and craving this party since we hatched the plan. Jon invited 20 guy friends of his — I didn't even know he knew 20 guys — and they're all attending the party planning to fuck me. They understand it's not required. No one's going to be checking a list — let alone checking it twice — and if they get here and aren't in the mood, they're welcome to stay and not partake of the offered goodies.

But most of them want what we're offering because I'm hot. I can finally admit that after feeling awkward and uncertain about myself for so long. With my long, wavy brown hair, big blue eyes, and curvy figure, I fit the definition of a hot wife. Over the years, Jon's friends kept telling him how lucky he is to fuck me all he wants, and now he's extending his good fortune to them. According to him, everyone coming to the party is incredibly eager, which surprises me since I didn't think he'd be able to find five takers of the offer, let alone 20.

CHAPTER 2

When I wake up the morning of the party, my pussy is a dripping mess and I stay in bed thinking about tonight. Jon bought extra lube, but I doubt it will be needed. The party doesn't start until evening. What in the hell am I going to do with myself all day? Shit, why didn't I plan a spa morning or a pedicure? I glance down at my painted red toes peeking out from under the blanket, wiggling them and eying them critically. Yeah, I don't need a pedicure yet.

Spreading my legs, I slide one hand underneath the band of my panties and and moan as I brush my fingers against my clit. If Jon were here with me, I would try for some morning sex because I'm already worked up. Plus, it's a good way to kill an hour and sets the right mood for the day. What's not to like about the idea? Unfortunately, his side of the bed is cold, so I know he's been up for a while.

Jon told me last night that he was getting up early to get stuff ready for tonight. He did all the organizing for the party and told me I only had to show up with bells on. I don't have bells, but now that I think of it, I should figure out what I'm wearing tonight, which will take all of five minutes. I really was poor at planning anything like this. It's been so long since I've done something out of the confines of my marriage that I forgot I always need plans in the morning for my usual day-of jitters.

My fingers are creating a swirl of pleasure and I close my eyes, ready to give in and go for it on my own when Jon walks in. When he notices me awake but hasn't realized yet what I'm doing under the covers, he exclaims, "Oh, hey!" I open my eyes and smile at him but don't remove my hand from my pussy.

He pauses when he figures out what I'm doing, and chuckles. "I see you're already getting warmed up for the party."

I'm breathy from being turned on, so I try to amp up the sex appeal and purr at him. "Mmm, maybe you should join me?"

Jon stands there, looking as if he's debating the offer, and my heart skips from excitement. Fuck yeah, morning sex here we come!

"No, Kitten. What's going to happen is you're going to stop touching yourself. You aren't allowed to come until tonight."

Uh, wait... what? His announcement causes me to stop the movement of my hand and I feel wetness dripping down my slit towards my ass. I'm immediately turned on even more and desperate to finger fuck myself to oblivion.

I pout at him. "You can't just decide like that, can you?"

The throbbing of my pussy tells me he can, and that I'll obey his order.

Jon flashes me an evil, sexy grin. "Unless you want me to call off the party, I think I can."

Ugh, fuck. I withdraw my fingers from underneath my panties and bring both hands outside the blanket, waving them in the air to prove I'm not touching myself. I mock glare at him, so turned on and yet suddenly cranky as well. This is what I get for making BDSM agreements with my husband. We don't have a 24/7 dominant-submissive relationship, but this party is part of our playtime and the fantasy has me in a submissive role, so he's in charge today. Despite how needy I am, I'm so fucking down for all of this and it's going to make tonight even better.

Jon walks over to me, leans down, brushes his lips against mine, and whispers, "Good girl."

My brain pings with pleasure from the endearment, and I resist the urge to pull him down onto the bed as he stands back up. I've found out the hard way that he's learned how to tame my inner brat, and I don't want to do anything to risk my party tonight.

I really do need to find something to do today, though, so I question him, hopeful. "Do you want any help with the party?"

"Nope, I only came in here to see if you were awake because I made cinnamon rolls and the coffee is fresh."

Oooh, he made me cinnamon rolls! Warmth spreads through my chest and any residual crankiness fades. He knows the way to my heart.

"Thank you, my love. I will come out and get some in a minute."

Jon smiles down at me, cups my cheek, and brushes a finger across my lower lip.

"Why don't you go shopping today and buy yourself a new toy?"

My pussy perks up at the idea, assuming he means a sex toy. I playfully try to bite his thumb and reply, "I might just do that."

"Well, make sure you're home by 5. I'm heading to the store for some party supplies, so you better behave and not touch yourself when I leave." He's stern, but winks at me at the end of his demand.

Nodding my head at him, I reply, "I'll be good. I promise."

Since it's not quite 9 a.m. I highly doubt I'm going to have a problem being home by 5, but I don't say anything more as I watch him walk out of the bedroom. Jesus, how did I get so lucky to find him?

CHAPTER 3

After a gooey, delicious cinnamon roll and some coffee, I toss on sweat-pants and a t-shirt. I'll take a shower before the party so there's no point in dressing up right now. No one's going to judge me at the sex toy store.

The lot at the strip mall is bustling, and it's hard to find a spot to park. Seems like everyone is out holiday shopping this morning. As soon as I walk into the shop, I see the toy I want. They have a holiday display and several of the items are vibrating ones that connect to an app for partner play. Oh, fuck yeah. I'm going to buy something that Jon and I will use together so this won't be only for me. I choose a large wand toy, thinking I might torture him and brush the underside of his cock with it to make him beg. Everything on the table is buy one, get one 50 percent off, and who can resist that deal?

After a brief perusal of the offerings, I spot a red-striped dildo, made of glass and shaped to look like a candy cane. Imagining holding on to the curved end and playing with it tickles my fancy, so I decide it will be my discount item. And really, it's the holidays, so everyone deserves a candy cane dildo.

At the checkout stand, there's a table of white and red striped thigh-highs that I can't resist, so I add that to my growing stash. The guy at the cash register is friendly and we make small talk about Christmas shopping while he rings up my purchases. When he suggests some pepper-mint-flavored lube, I giggle and it gets added into the bag as well. Might as well, since I've got a theme going on.

When I get out to the car, I pull out the see-through box with the glass dildo visible, snap a picture of it, and send it to my husband with a Christmas tree emoji. I barely have my seatbelt buckled when my phone rings and Jon's picture pops up on the lock screen to show he's the one calling me.

"Um, hello?" I'm confused when I answer, but I assume he needs me to pick up ice or some other item he forgot at the store.

He doesn't give any pleasantries and immediately asks, "You're still parked, right?"

Uh, what's this? "Yeah... why?"

Jon's voice is commanding when he states. "Okay, Kitten, listen closely. I'm still at the store, but you're going to take that candy cane out of the box, shove it in your pussy and and play with yourself for exactly three minutes."

Holy fuck. My entire body lights up and my breath catches, but he continues on.

"Then you're going to drive home with it inside you, park the car in the garage, and send me a picture of it in you as proof you did what I asked."

Jon and I are decently kinky, but this is a little more than we've done lately, and I'm loving it. My pussy is wet and throbbing and I softly reply, "Yes, sir."

"Good girl. Now do your task and I expect the picture in 15 minutes."

When he hangs up, I stare at the phone dumbly for a few seconds before realizing 15 minutes doesn't give me much time since it includes driving time. I fumble with the box, and when I pull out the dildo I realize I have two problems. First, I'm wearing sweatpants, so this won't be as easy as a skirt. And second, I'm not shoving some unwashed item up there.

I paw through the glove box and find some wet wipes to solve one problem. I quickly wipe the glass toy down, enjoying the heaviness of it. This isn't a cheaply made item, but I run my hands all over it, searching for cracks or any defects. It's smooth and perfect, and I'm so wet I know it's going to slide right in once I settle the sweatpants issue.

Glancing around the parking lot, I wait until no one is approaching the cars next to me and lift my ass off the seat and pull my sweatpants and panties down to my knees. I can't remove them any further unless I want to be naked on my bottom half because I need full movement of my feet for driving. I'm able to spread my knees just enough to slide the candy cane between my legs and nudge the entrance of my pussy.

I set a timer on my phone in case I get too involved and press the toy all the way inside me, keeping the curved end up as a handle. Three minutes won't get me there, but it'll be a good tease. He knows this about me and I'm positive that's why he said three minutes exactly.

I slowly fuck myself with the candy cane and fight the urge to lean back against the seat and close my eyes. I moan softly and keep watch to make sure no poor unsuspecting person tries to get into the car next to mine. Spikes of pleasure shoot through my core as I speed up my thrusts.

The timer going off jolts me, and I swear. Fuck. I half hate my husband at this moment, but I'm also totally in love with him at the same time. He knows exactly how to torture me. I leave the cane in and start the car, being careful to concentrate on the road. If it were a vibrating toy, I'd have more problems, but the dildo sits inside me all snug, leaving me needy and aching for more as I drive home.

When I park the car in the garage, I take a picture showing as much of the candy cane as I can. With the curved end pointed towards my stomach, there is no doubt it's in my pussy. I include a kiss emoji when I hit send, and he responds with three flames.

Pulling the toy out of me, I shove it in its box and head into the house with my goodies.

CHAPTER 4

The rest of the day goes by quickly. Jon comes home and I convince him to let me help prep some of the food items, and before I know it, I need to take my shower and get ready. I want to be comfortable tonight, so after I dry off, I put on a pair of black shorts, a red t-shirt, and pull out my new red and white striped thigh-highs. Might as well be festive until it's time to get naked.

After my tease this morning and thinking about the party all day long, I might explode with the first cock inside me at this rate. I'm ready for the big night with a little over an hour to spare, so I wander around the house, fussing with the holiday decorations and making sure everything looks like a normal household. Somehow this matters. They're coming over to use me, but in my head I want them to think my house seems like any other household. Because clearly, Jon and I are a normal couple where the wife has a "being used" kink. Nothing out of the ordinary — nope, nothing at all.

I wander around the house looking for things to straighten, and when I get into the kitchen I peek at the guest list laid out on the counter. Jon has mentioned about three-fourths of the guys on it, but there are a few names I'm unfamiliar with, which electrifies me. Since my fantasy includes being blindfolded, I won't know who is fucking me, but the idea that some of the men will be total strangers gives me a naughty zing. I'm so preoccupied with the list, I don't notice when Jon walks in.

He clears his throat and I glance towards the doorway where he's standing. He announces with a soft smile, "Miranda, it's time."

My stomach clenches in a knot and I fight the urge to run, telling myself I'm an idiot. This is literally my idea, and Jon would call it off in a heartbeat if I asked. But I don't wish that. I want to see this through. This is my ultimate fantasy and I'm so close to having it fulfilled.

He leads me to the rec room, turns to me and tells me to strip. Shit, he's not wasting any time, and an excited knot forms in my stomach. I watch Jon arrange a red folded blanket on the coffee table next to the bowl of condoms, and he puts a standard bedroom pillow down on top.

When he notices I'm still standing there watching him, he gives me "the look" which means I'm dawdling, and I hurriedly strip off my shorts, t-shirt, and underclothes. When I start to roll one of the thigh-highs down my leg, he stops me.

"No, leave those on."

Fuck, yeah! I love how thigh-highs look, and imagining myself being trussed up while wearing them is a sexy visual. I smooth it back up my leg, and he takes the rest of my clothes from me. He sets them on the floor next to the couch in a neat pile, while picking up some green bondage rope at the same time. Of course, Jon would make the rope match the theme. He's such a goof.

Jon commands, "Put your hands behind your back," and a thrill runs through me, straight to my pussy.

I do as I'm told, and Jon expertly secures my wrists behind me with a double column tie. When he's done, he moves the pillow and pats the blanket, indicating he wants me to get up on the coffee table. I kneel on the surface, and my pussy is so wet, I swear my juices are dripping down my inner thigh. *Fuck, this is insanely hot.*

My life now versus how it was a couple of years ago always startles me with the difference. I remember when Jon first got interested in bondage and didn't know what he was doing. After some lessons, he's tying me up regularly with expertise, and we both enjoy it. I love being tied up and at the mercy of whatever he wants to do to me, so it wasn't a big leap to realize I have a kink about being used.

Jon bends down for a deep kiss, and part of me wishes it was just us tonight. I know this experience is going to be amazing, but I'm a little scared and I love Jon so much. I don't want to ruin what we have with my perverted fantasy. We fought so hard to get to where we are today, it almost seems stupid to risk our happiness over an unnecessary wish fulfillment.

Since we started planning this, he's told me repeatedly how much he wants it too, and how turned on he is by the idea, but I'm still afraid it will change things. How many guys would be okay with their wife being used by multiple men while they watch? Probably not a lot.

When he breaks off the kiss, he frog ties my thigh and ankle together on the right side, forcing my leg to stay in a kneeling position, and then moves to do the same to the left. He and I have done bondage play often enough that none of this is unfamiliar or uncomfortable. I know by the time he releases me, it won't feel that great, but that adds to the excitement.

Once he's finished, he sets the pillow in front of me on the coffee table and bends me over so my head is comfortable on the cushion and my nipples brush against the blanket creating a delicious tingle. I'm kneeling with my ass up in the air. Anyone behind me is going to get a full view of my dripping pussy and tight asshole.

I'm not sure how much time we have before people arrive, but I'm almost ready. The only thing left to put on is the blindfold — or so I thought. Jon pulls out a Santa hat from underneath a pillow on the couch, like he was hiding it, and he sets it on my head. I giggle while he stands back and judges the effect critically.

"Yep, that will do," he announces in an amused tone.

Jon lays a black silk blindfold over my eyes and secures it at the back of my head, making sure to re-adjust the Santa hat when he's done. Being plunged into darkness sends a rush through my core. *Holy shit.* From this point on, I won't know whose cock will be inside me.

I hear a clinking like a belt buckle from behind me, and Jon asks, "Kitten, you okay?"

My voice is soft when I answer, "Yes, love, I'm fine."

"Good, because I plan on being the first one to fuck you tonight."

As soon as he says that, the tip of his cock probes the entrance of my cave and I moan out as he pushes in fully. He never mentioned this in the plan, but now that he's doing it, I realize how perfect it is. I've said all along that I don't want tonight to be about my pleasure because the fantasy is that I'm being used, and as Jon fucks me hard and fast, I can tell he's taking me at my word.

Since I've been so turned on all day, it doesn't take much to ramp me towards an orgasm and I'm squealing with each thrust while I lie there helpless. Jon groans loudly and, with a final jerk, he unloads his hot sticky cum deep inside me. *Fuuuuck, I was so close to coming.*

He pulls out just as the doorbell rings, and he laughs. "Good timing. It's show time."

I hear a rustle behind me, as if he's pulling his jeans up and zipping them, and then the coat closet door squeaks open and something is dragged across the floor. *What the fuck is that?* I sense he's walked away out of the rec room.

I don't know what to expect, and as I perch there, panting, I can feel his cum sliding out of me and down my leg. *Jesus, this is obscene.* Knowing how I probably look is keeping me at a high state of alert to any sound in case someone sneaks into the room.

I hear laughter and chatting in the kitchen, and I can't tell how many people arrived. The doorbell rings constantly for a while but no one comes into the rec room. The longer I'm by myself, the more anxious I become.

Our agreement was that Jon would be with me the entire time in case I freaked out. So where is he?

Eventually, Jon comes back. "You still doing okay?"

I want to get cranky and accuse him of leaving me, but I only say, "Yes." The almost-funny, horrible part about it is that the longer I was alone, the more turned on I got. Thinking that someone could sneak in and start fucking me at any moment without Jon here was just the right mix of scary and exciting.

I hear the stereo turn on and familiar holiday music blasts out. "Santa Baby" by Eartha Kitt makes me smile and I wiggle my ass a little in time with the song. The music seems to be the key to drawing people in, and before long, multiple men are chatting behind me. My husband settles down on the couch in front of me, and occasionally touches my face or pets my hair.

"You're doing so good, Miranda. I won't leave again. Let me know if you need anything or want to stop."

Knowing he's right there calms me a little. There are obviously people in the room, but no one approaches me, and wondering if they are all staring at my pussy keeps me wet. Jon's cum is drying on my leg, and I wonder how long it will be before someone gets brave.

Jon wanders off to help a friend find a different holiday song and eventually someone comes up behind me. I don't know who it is, but a hand caresses my buttocks and I jump from the unexpected contact.

"Uh, I can just stick it in?"

Once the person speaks, I know it's Jon's best friend, Steve, whom I actually had a hotwife experience with, so I've fucked him before.

"Yep." Jon sounds almost cheerful when he replies from behind me. Is he standing back there watching?

Steve is nice enough to ask me. "Miranda, you're okay with this?"

I don't bother pretending I don't know who he is. "Yes, Steve. Fuck me."

My slutty words create an inferno in my belly, and I hope he's rough with me. I hear someone, who I assume is Steve, rifle in the condom bowl and a packet rips open. A moment later, a cock eases into me. As he slowly pumps in and out, I'm disappointed yet still turned on. He's nowhere near as violent as I'd like, but each stroke hits a sensitive point that elicits a moan. It doesn't take long before he groans and presses against me before pulling out.

"Fuck, that was good. Thank you," he states as he walks away.

I don't reply to him, and I sense Jon sitting down on the couch in front of me. He cups my chin, brushing his thumb across my lower lip, then leans in and whispers in my ear, "I love you," and kisses me softly on the cheek.

Steve's bravery broke the ice. Jon gets up to help someone else with something and it's only a minute before another guy is at my ass. This time I can't tell who it is by the voice, but he brings the hard thrusts I am craving. I cry out with each whack against my sodden hole, which grabs the attention of the entire room. Soon everyone is cheering the guy on, as I inch closer and closer to my orgasm.

This is all so fabulously slutty, and I can't believe all these people are watching me get pounded. That thought drives me over the edge, and I scream out as I come. Waves of pleasure wash over me while he keeps fucking me relentlessly.

When Mr. Hard Thrusting finally comes, I realize he never put on a condom as his thick ropes of cum paint my cave walls. We said on the invitation that condoms were optional, and I was curious how many guys would take us up on that offer. Thinking about another man's spunk in me makes a shiver run down my spine from how dirty it is.

After that, it's a parade of men behind me with small breaks in between. I lose track of my orgasms after the fourth. Some voices I recognize, others I don't, but I don't know if people were visiting my pussy multiple times or if it was only once for whoever wanted. Most of the guys only pumped in and out a couple of times before pulling out, and some only fingered and played with my clit. I tried to count the number of condoms that were used, but things blurred together after a while. Even the cocks all started to feel the same.

I reach a point where I zone out while I'm mentally floating and everything is dreamlike and wonderful. Jon keeps coming to sit in front of me and check in with me, caressing my face and giving me kisses. A few times he brings a bottle of water and helps me prop up so he can put it to my lips while I take greedy sips. All the moaning is making my throat dry.

I can tell my Santa hat is askew, and the thought makes me giggle. I'm like some weird tied-up Christmas gift for anyone to enjoy. At least my fantasy didn't include spit roasting. That would have been an even funnier sight. Jon's being so loving and caring. He really is the best husband ever.

I don't know how much time had passed when Jon ushers everyone out of the room and I hear the door connecting the den to the hallway click closed. It might have been one hour, it could have been three hours since the party started.

I'm in a sexual daze and barely notice Jon untying me. My pussy is a swirl of cum and my juices but it seems like most guys wore condoms. I'm not sure if that was a good thing or a bad thing, but I was right, and I didn't need any lube.

Jon takes my blindfold off and I blink at him as he picks me up off the coffee table and lays me down on the floor next to our Christmas tree, slipping the pillow behind my head. I stare up at the twinkling lights as he covers my body with his. He sucks on my nipples briefly, making me gasp before slipping his cock inside me, stretching me one final time. I whimper softly as he fucks me hard. This part was in the plan. He told me he wanted to be the last person to come in me tonight.

Jon's voice is harsh. "Who owns you?"

I moan out, "You do. Only you."

He's rough, and I thought I couldn't orgasm anymore tonight, but I am suddenly rushing towards the peak again.

With each sharp thrust, he questions me with something new and demands a response.

"Who is the only person you want to fill you with cum?"

"You. Only you!"

"Who's my dirty little slut?"

"Me!"

"Who is the one who made this all happen for you?"

"You. You did!"

"Do you still love me?"

I scream out "Yes!" and come so hard the room spins, as spikes of pleasure radiate all the way to my toes and fingers. Jon bucks wildly against me and roars as he comes. He fills me with everything he's got left as I quiver underneath him.

I'm barely coherent when he pulls out and cuddles up next to me, drawing me close and murmuring how wonderful I am. I'm dazed and through the fog I realize my lack of response is concerning him.

I murmur, "I love you so much, Jon. Thank you."

He kisses my shoulder and pulls me tighter against him. "You're welcome, Kitten. I love you too."

I blink and scan the empty room. There's a privacy screen set up around the coffee table, and I smile tiredly. That must have been what I heard being dragged from the closet. I'll have to ask him later where he got it from because it was a great idea. I'm glad I didn't know that part of the plan. Thinking everyone could see every inch of me took the fantasy to a whole other level.

Jon and I lay wrapped in each other's arms, and I almost doze off when Jon asks.

"Was that authentic enough that you felt like you were living out your fantasy?"

I yawn loudly and giggle, thinking about how much organizing this all took for Jon to make it seem real. "Oh, God, yes."

Jon kisses my shoulder again. "Good. Everyone had a script and a schedule. I have some pretty amazing friends to help me out with this."

I'm embarrassed for a moment, thinking about his friends. But I already fucked Steve once on a bet so I could get a Hawaiian vacation out of Jon so it's not like Steve didn't know I was kinky.

I'm alarmed at my next thought, tense up, and blurt out. "Wait, Steve didn't really fuck me, did he?"

Jon pulls me closer to him. "No, Kitten. That was me every single time tonight, just like we planned all along."

I relax into his arms again. Jesus, my husband is a rock star.

The multiple discarded condom packages on the floor catch my attention. "Uh, how many times did you come?"

Jon laughs. "Three times. That's why some of the 'guys' didn't fuck you long."

My brain is a little more awake now, so I'm curious about the details. "How many guys were actually here?"

"About 15 showed up. Steve has a recording of background noise at a party to make it sound like more people were here if we needed, but enough wandered in and out that we didn't use it."

All of Jon's friends are aware of our lifestyle and no one strong-armed them into helping, so they must be all cool with it. I blush and squirm against Jon, thinking about all of them hearing me moaning. This experience hit part of my humiliation kink, so it thrills me and embarrasses me at the same time. Knowing other people listened is hot, but thank God they weren't also watching. I wouldn't be able to look them in the eye again. But shit, I think one of them has a holiday party coming up that we agreed to go to. This is going to make the initial greeting at the party a little awkward.

The level of detail it took to bring this fantasy of mine to life is amazing. Jon loves to do research, and this probably amused his brain, but he put in a lot of hard work to make it believable enough for my mind to think there really were different men fucking me.

I sigh contentedly, and cuddle with Jon while his cum leaks out of me and my pussy throbs from how long and hard he fucked me tonight. It all gives me that delicious used feeling I craved, and knowing it was only my husband inside of me and he arranged this all so I could fulfill my fantasy safely, makes me love him more.

I'm about to fall asleep right there on the floor and to keep myself awake, I ask Jon. "What is your biggest fantasy? Is it something I can help with?"

Jon laughs and since I'm snuggled so close to him, the vibrations rumble through his chest.

"Kitten, all those months of hotwife stuff was my biggest fantasy, and you already fulfilled it. I'm just happy being with you."

Oh, right… that. I enjoyed being a hotwife as well, so it's easy to forget it was his fantasy to begin with.

We drift for a bit, and I know things will never be quite the same, but this wish fulfillment went better than I imagined. Eventually he carries me to bed and as I snuggle under the covers, I think that my life feels pretty complete right now. But who knows what fabulously slutty thing my brain will come up with next. I just know that even if this was my only Christmas gift this year, I wouldn't complain. My bells are well jingled and, unlike Santa, I get to come more than once per year.

The End

NEEDING HER THAT NIGHT

CHAPTER 1

I tap my pen on the counter and scan my comic book store to make sure there aren't any customers needing anything. The main sales floor isn't large, but we have several side rooms and the largest is bustling. I've spent most of the night sitting on a stool behind the counter, bored out of my mind. Usually I text my wife during my downtime late at night, but my wife, Mindy, is staying at her sister's tonight helping with wedding planning. They're probably busy so I don't want to bother them. At 39, her sister is younger than she is, and getting married in a couple of weeks — for the fifth time. Her fiancé seems like a good egg, so I hope this one sticks. Everyone deserves some happiness in life.

When I was a kid, it was my dream to own a comic book store when I grew up, and sure, I'm living the dream, but it isn't turning out like I pictured. First off, I'm not wealthy. In my head, when I was younger, I always assumed people who owned any type of store were rich, but apparently that's not how it goes in the comic book store business. I make a decent income, but I won't be retiring at age 50, that's for certain. Another thing I didn't anticipate when I was a kid was that to make money, you need to offer a variety of options. We provide gaming rooms people can use because it gets them in the door, and then they stay and buy our products.

We also have an area of computers that people can rent by the hour for LAN parties — or hell, just to do their homework if they want.

A couple of months ago I hired Josh, a punk guy in his early 20s with no real life ambition yet, but he's a wiz with computers and keeps them updated and running smoothly for me. Josh enjoys working Friday nights, so he's the only other employee here with me. We stay open late on Fridays for a trading card game tournament and it's after midnight already. I always let Josh go home before me. No point in making both of us wait for the games to finish.

Josh comes out of the computer room, closes the door behind him, and locks it with his key. He's lanky and slightly unkempt, but not enough to bug the customers. He saunters over to me, coming around to the back of the counter, and opens the drawer under the cash register to grab his paycheck.

"Eli, I'm heading out. I've got a hot date with a sleek pink-haired pixie."

I smile at him, knowing he probably doesn't have a date unless the pixie is in an online multiplayer game. But it's possible, who knows? He wasn't eager to leave tonight though, so it can't be that hot.

"Have a good night, Josh. I'll see you on Monday."

Josh salutes me on his way out the door, and the bells on the handle jingle as the door bounces a few times before settling closed. I got a great deal on an old building that used to be a small theater. It was sectioned off into various areas before I bought it, and it suits my needs perfectly. The ornate molding on the walls creates a creepy effect if I dim all the lights, and sometimes a shiver runs down my spine. In the dark, the store is the type of old building ghosts would haunt.

I mentally cheer when I can tell the tournament is almost over. A few people start leaving, and it's a chorus of goodbyes since I know everyone's name by heart. It's the same group of people who show up week after week: mostly guys in their 40s, like me, who played the game when they were teenagers.

I tap my pen on the counter again, wishing the last players would hurry up and leave when the pen jumps out of my hand and does a spinning flip, arching over my shoulder and landing on the floor behind me. I couldn't have recreated that if I tried. Hopefully the security camera caught it so I can watch the action again later. Snorting in amusement, I lean down to pick it up as the bells on the door jingle and I fumble with the pen as it rolls further out of my reach. I almost have to get on my hands and knees to retrieve it from under the counter.

When I straighten up, my heart stops and my breath catches in my throat. Holy fuck. Right In front of me is the backside of a woman browsing a shelf of board games, and I swear it's the ghost of my wife's past because the outfit she has on is almost identical to my favorite thing my wife used to wear when I met her 23 years ago.

She's wearing a short, ruffled black skirt and a long-sleeved black top. The deep purple corset with lace ties in the back is the part I remember best. My fingers itch to pull the ribbons loose, remembering how I always felt like I was unwrapping Mindy when I took it off of her. The woman's black hair is in a topknot and I see streaks of purple in it. Tall black motorcycle boots with zippers up the side complete the outfit.

My body responds as if she were my partner, and my cock grows hard in my jeans. Oh shit, that's just what I need. I'm getting horny over a customer. It's possible she's picking someone up for the tournament, but I don't want to bug her and make assumptions. My brain is playing tricks on me and still thinks it's Mindy, but I know it can't be. For one thing, Mindy doesn't have black hair. She has beautiful chestnut curls, and this lady's hair is an updo but I can tell her hair is straight. Mindy hasn't colored her hair black since we went through our goth phase a decade and a half ago. That was long before the kids were born, and I prefer her natural color now.

But I know it can't be. Mindy hasn't fit into that outfit for years. Heck, I don't even know if she still has it. Last time I saw it was maybe five years ago when she pulled it out and got all nostalgic over wishing she could wear it again. Three kids and 20-odd years makes that impossible. This last year, getting healthy has been the focus for the two of us and we've both lost significant weight, but I don't think Mindy is small enough yet to wear those clothes again.

Mindy will never believe some woman showed up looking like she did years ago. I wish I could pull out my phone and take a picture, but that would be creepy. I shift on my stool, trying to rearrange my junk without touching myself like a perv. The longer I look at the woman, the more I notice subtle differences between her and my vision of younger Mindy. This woman's lush curves strain the fabric of the outfit in the most perfect way. Mindy had a small frame until she had children and gained weight.

I love my wife's body though, and there's nothing wrong with more to hold on to and cuddle with. Snuggling with Mindy and resting my head on her squishy belly while she runs her fingers through my hair is absolute heaven. I've joked with her that I don't want her to get too thin because I adore her softness. She always laughs and assures me that won't happen. We enjoy taco Tuesdays and pizza Fridays too much for either of us to be as thin as our old selves ever again.

The thoughts of my wife from the past war with the woman in front of me. She's browsing the shelves, but every movement reminds me of Mindy, and I'm getting an odd sense of déjà vu. The room grows hot and the crazy thought pops into my head that I need to go into the stockroom and stroke one out before I leave for the night. I don't know the last time I masturbated at work, but tonight it's happening. Since Mindy is gone, there is no point in rushing home for anything. I've had a fantasy of fucking a customer at my store, and this woman's reminder of Mindy from the past has created a need inside me.

After the store closes, I'll go into the back room and picture Mindy as a customer. Maybe she'll even be wearing that old outfit of hers. I'll push Fantasy Mindy up against the wall and fuck her hard until she screams out my name. I've asked Mindy to come in and roleplay like she's a customer in the past, but she only laughs and says she'd rather stay home, naked in our soft bed, and wait for me to get off work. Fuck, I need to stop thinking about this until the shop is empty.

I try to shake off the lust raging through my system, but when the goth woman bends over at the waist to look at something on a lower shelf, I almost groan. Her ass is directly in my line of sight, as if it was planned. My cock throbs in my pants and I haven't been this turned on in years. We had our three kids later in life, so they're still pretty young — the oldest is six — and that doesn't leave much time for sex anymore. We've hit a bit of a dry patch lately, and I'd hoped getting into shape would revitalize our love life, but so far it hasn't.

The last of the tournament players finally pack up and the winners stop at the front desk for their reward booster packs. A few guys pause and murmur among each other, staring at the curvy figure of the goth woman. She doesn't acknowledge any of them and when I hear a comment about the hot woman that's loud enough to reach her ears, I'm sharp when I tell people it's time to go. They head out the door with a chorus of "Goodbye, Eli," but the woman doesn't leave with them.

What's going on here? My cock keeps getting ideas that it shouldn't be having and now it looks like I'll have to talk to her since she's still browsing the shelves. I need her to go so I can lock up and continue my fantasy of fucking my 20-year-old wife.

"Uh, I'm sorry, but the shop is closing. Can I help you find something really quick?"

The woman finally turns towards me and the room spins while my heart pounds.

Uh… what the fuck? It IS Mindy.

She walks up to the counter, smiles at me through her heavy makeup and purrs, "I don't know. I seem to have an itch that needs to be scratched. Can you help me?"

I feel my mouth drop open and my mind drains of all thoughts while my cock strains against my pants.

She leans an elbow on the countertop and runs a black-painted fingernail up the back of my hand.

"Is there a problem? Aren't you supposed to always satisfy the customer?" She pauses for a moment, and her tongue slips out of her mouth. She licks her lips and continues. "My name's Cassara. What's yours?"

A flush of warmth from my groin travels up my body. Cassara is the name she used when we used to vampire LARP. She's still running her finger along my skin, and I capture her hand. I hold her hand up, and use my other hand to rub circles on her palm, knowing whenever I do that it always turns her on. I stare into her eyes, watching them glaze over with longing as I caress her.

I have the most amazing wife in the world. She did this all for me. She must have been over at her sister's coloring her hair and getting dressed up tonight. I hadn't realized she'd lost this much weight because we mostly lounge around in loose clothes that are too big for us now, but she still has her curves and is smoking hot.

The sudden urge for this to be the best sex of her life hits me. She went through a ton of effort to do this and is fulfilling one of my fantasies. Now it's my turn to make her glad she did. The thought brings me back in control and while the lust haze is still present, I'm focused on my wife and her pleasure.

I lift her hand to my mouth and kiss her soft skin, telling her, "Cassara is the perfect name for such a beautiful woman."

She grins at me when I call her Cassara and I can tell she's pleased that I'm willing to play along.

"So Cassara, about this itch. Why don't you come into the back room with me and show me where it is so I can help you?"

She giggles, and it warms my heart. I love her laugh, and some nights I spam her instant messenger with cute pet pictures and happy babies just to keep her giggling.

I move around the counter and walk over to double check that everyone is out of the gaming room. Cassara waits for me as I lock the front door and turn off the open sign. I hold out my hand to her and she slides her palm against mine. Little pings of pleasure run up my arm from her touch. This is the same woman I've been sleeping next to for years, but adding in a little roleplay makes the slightest touch more arousing.

I say, "Come with me," and lead her to the back of the shop.

CHAPTER 2

As we enter the stockroom, she pauses. "You never told me your name. Maybe I shouldn't be back here with a strange man?"

Turning to face her, I try to hide my smile. "I'm so sorry. Your beauty distracted me. I'm Jules."

Of course, that's my vampire name from years ago. Her eyes twinkle. "Well, Jules. Let me get more comfortable and I'll show you exactly where the itch is."

Our banter would sound totally stupid to anyone overhearing us, but in the moment, it's fucking hot. I want to rip off her clothes, bend her over the closest surface, and hammer away at her pussy. But I need to keep my calm and make sure she gets a fabulous orgasm before I come.

In my workplace fantasy, it was always me using the customer with no regard for her pleasure, but doing this with my wife is better than anything I had in my head and I don't want to simply use her. She needs to be fully satisfied and limp like a dishrag when I'm done with her. Years from now, I want her to remember how awesome tonight was.

Cassara bends over to unzip her boots and I admire the way her breasts overflow the top of her corset. She kicks the boots aside and pulls off her socks. Her toes match her black-painted fingernails and I admire the delicate arches of her feet. I've kissed those toes and the arches a thousand times as I lifted them up to my shoulders before thrusting into her, but the black polish brings back memories of the past, when I explored her body for the first time. She didn't need to remove the socks, but she did it for me because she knows I love her tiny, sexy feet.

She pauses for a minute and we lock eyes before she reaches behind her to undo the button and small zipper on her skirt. I hold back a groan. This just turned into a nice striptease. I lean against the old ticket counter from when this was a theater and enjoy the show.

When the skirt drops to the floor, my mouth goes dry and a sexual tingle runs through me. She's wearing black satin and lace panties, and my cock throbs in response. God, my wife is so fucking gorgeous and sexy. I yearn to fill my hands and mouth with her delectable body, but I want her to be in control for the moment until I take it away from her. She's enjoying her effect on me, and she's flushed and breathing hard so I know it's making her hot.

I reach down and stroke myself through my jeans to show her how much I'm appreciating everything she's doing. Her eyes follow my hand for a moment as she steps out of the skirt and pushes it to the side with her foot. When I realize she's about to reach behind her and undo the corset, I spring into action. *Oh hell no, that's my job.*

"Stop," I growl at her.

When she halts with her hands at her back, I tell her. "Turn around."

Her lips part and her eyes widen as she silently faces the wall. The satin and lace of her panties stretch across her full ass and when I press up against her, I caress each cheek and lean down to nibble on her neck. She tips her head to the side and moans. "God, Jules, that feels so good."

I move my mouth up and tug at an earlobe and she giggles. I know it's a sensitive spot that both tickles and turns her on. When I whisper in her ear, "Spread your legs a little," she immediately complies and I get a nice ping of pleasure from her obeying my command. In the past, she and I have experimented with BDSM since I enjoy being in control during sex, but it was never anything we did seriously. In the last few years, we've been too busy to explore much in the bedroom, but tonight, my almost overwhelming desire to fuck her roughly tells me we need to make more time. This is exactly what's been missing lately.

Running my hand between her legs from behind, I caress her pussy through the fabric of her panties. She groans and leans back against me. The delicate panties are already wet, and I press firmly against them, straining the material as I rub her.

I bite her neck softly and ask, "Cassara, how do you want me to fuck you?"

"Oh," she peeps out in a small voice, and just that one word tells me she's reached the point where she's sexually dazed and not able to think.

She sighs as she answers. "Bent over the table, please."

I smile, knowing she can't see it, and slip my finger underneath the edge of her panties so I can fondle her.

"Too bad, sluts don't get to decide. I want you against the wall."

I make sure my fingers are slick with her wetness before I caress her clit in circles. She rewards me with a moan and I bite down harder on her neck. She gasps as my teeth dig in deep enough to brand her. If she goes over to her sister's house tomorrow, I want her squirming and hiding the mark to avoid having to endure a day's worth of her sister's teasing comments.

Kissing my way up to her ear again, I nibble on her earlobe and she shivers while I rub gentle circles against her swollen bean. My cock is rock hard and I'm close to losing control, so I remove my fingers from her pussy and take a step back so I can unwrap my present.

I croon at her, trying to contrast my harsh bite with softness to make her head spin. "Cassara, you're so pretty, all wrapped up like a gift. The perfect little slut who walked into my store and offered herself to me in this gorgeous package."

When I brush my fingers against the bare skin at the back of her neck, tracing the collar of her shirt, she responds with a soft murmur. I know my wife, and I'm not sure she's capable of speech right now. Her sighs and shivering tell me she'll do whatever I ask of her. Shit, it's been far too long since we've done anything like this.

Taking a calming, deep breath, I focus on the stays of her corset. I pluck at the bow at the bottom edge, untying it slowly, loosening the ribbons, freeing one side as I move up her back. When it's undone, I drop the corset on top of her discarded skirt and turn her around to face me.

Her lips are parted and she's breathing heavily, so I cup her cheek and brush my thumb along her red-stained bottom lip. She used to wear black lipstick, but I think I prefer this dark red color.

I love her so much and want to make sure she's okay since I haven't seen her this worked up in quite some time.

"You doing okay, Cassara?"

She gives me a dreamy smile. "Yes, Jules. I'm fine."

I flash her my best wicked grin. "That's good, since I'm about to fuck you up."

Pressing her back against the wall, I pin both of her wrists above her head and swoop down to ravage her mouth. When she parts her lips for me, I slip my tongue between them. Just as I expected, she tastes of her favorite cinnamon gum. I've grown to love that flavor. We deepen the kiss and she arches against me, moaning against my mouth. I take my time, exploring her lips. When I finally fuck her, I want her to come so hard she sees stars, so I need to bring her to the edge first.

I grind against her as we continue our kiss. When we break apart, I groan because I'm too close to losing control again. I want to be inside her, feeling her silky folds caressing the length of my shaft, but it's not time yet.

Letting go of her wrists, I quickly remove her shirt, pulling it up over her head and tossing it on the growing pile of clothes. My shirt also joins it so I can feel her bare skin against my chest. She has a matching satin and lace bra on, and while I would love to admire her in it, I need those plump nipples in my mouth.

I press in close as I snake my hands behind her back, expertly unhook her bra, and let it drop on top of her corset. Her unbound breasts are heavy and full, and her pert nipples beg to be sucked. I wouldn't trade her body for her younger self. As she's aged, her boobs grew larger, and even more so since we had kids. They now overfill my palms and I love to play with them. Leaning down, I take a dusty rose nipple into my mouth and she sighs as I suck gently, swirling my tongue around the areola but always focusing back on the stiff peak. She weaves her hands in my hair while I switch breasts, making sure the other one doesn't feel left out.

I continue to suck on her nipples, alternating every few moments until she's pushing against me and moving her hips as if her pussy demands attention. Dropping to my knees, I slowly peel her panties down her legs and lift one of her feet up, forcing her knee to bend, and kissing the top of her foot as I slide the panties off. I do the same with the other and when both her feet are back on the floor, I start at her knee and kiss my way up her inner thighs.

She can tell she's enjoying what I'm doing, and she closes her eyes and spreads her legs as I get close to her pussy. Using both hands, I spread her nether lips and lean in for a taste. She moans as my tongue finds her clit. I'm not sure how much longer I can wait. My cock is painfully hard and it's leaking pre-cum. My jeans are going to be a mess at this rate, but I need a little more time to get Mindy to the brink.

I stop licking for a moment. "Is this where the itch is?"

"Oh, god, yes," she moans as I lean back in and eagerly lick her clit. When I slide a finger inside of her and massage against her cave wall, she gasps louder.

"Oooh, fuck. I'm going to come!" She grinds her pussy against my face and a splash of wetness hits me and I promptly clean it up. She hasn't come yet, but she's close enough. I press a second finger inside her wet box and when she squeals and tries to fuck my fingers, I know she's ready.

I stand up and kiss her deeply, forcing her to taste herself on my lips while I unbuckle my belt, unzip my jeans, and pull them down with my boxers. There's no time to remove them or my shoes. I need her right now.

I reach my hand down between her thighs, give her a final quick rub, and I'm rewarded with a groan. Hooking one of her legs around my hips, I hold on to it and slam my cock into her tight cave.

"Oooooh!" she cries out and shudders underneath me, but still doesn't come. This feels so fucking amazing and I want to turn into a wild beast, losing myself in her softness until I explode. With every thrust, she whimpers and pushes against me.

The need to verify she's mentally gone hits me, and I'm gruff when I command, "Cassara, look at me."

"Wha...?" She tries to focus on me, but I see her eyes roll back and I know she's beyond thought. I force my thumb into her mouth and she sucks on it, swirling her tongue to lick off any of her remaining juices while I speed up my strokes.

In and out... in and out... I become just as mindless as she is, and all I can think about is shooting my load deep inside her.

My balls tighten and I'm going to come soon, but I need to wait for her. I remove my thumb from her mouth and move my hand to brush against her clit. I'm not gentle this time and as I rub hard circles, she climaxes.

"Ooooh, my god!" She convulses against me, crying out as her pussy clenches while she grinds against my shaft.

Knowing she came pushes me over the edge and I make one final plunge and explode. I unload ropes of my cum deep inside her shuddering cave, and she's moaning and panting from her orgasm. Kissing her passionately, I'm gentle as I press against her, letting her pussy milk the last few drops of cum from me.

My kissing becomes softer while we both come down from our high. When we break apart, I slide my softening cock from her and release the thigh I've been holding up. I haphazardly pull up my jeans and boxers, and walk her over to the nearest chair.

Sitting down, I pull her into my lap, kissing her forehead and letting her lean her head against my shoulder as I wrap my arms around her. My head is reeling and I'm seeing stars. I have to smile at myself because I wanted to do that to her, but it's taking me a moment to come down from the intense high.

She relaxes against me, and I smile at her smeared lipstick. I'm sure I look a fright in the mirror right now because most of what is missing from her lips is on me.

"Mindy, you are so fucking amazing. Do you know that?"

She giggles and gives an "uh-huh," and I squeeze her tightly against me, rocking her. We're both sweaty, and I love the scent of our lovemaking on her skin.

A thought makes me pause the rocking. "Wait, where are the kids?"

Mindy outright laughs at my question. "They're with my sister. I got them settled down watching Beauty and the Beast. She'll call if there are any problems, but otherwise she said to enjoy the night and just come get them early tomorrow morning."

My cock attempts to spring to life at the thought of the rest of the night alone with my wife. I can't remember the last time we had this freedom without the kids. I bet by the time we get home, I'll be ready for round two.

I push her off my lap, slap her ass, and she squeals. "Let's take my car home. We'll pick yours up in the morning. I have the urge to get you nice and soapy in the shower, wash that makeup off you, and see how hard you can come a second time."

She looks over her shoulder at me and wiggles her ass a little. "Yes, Sir."

My cock stiffens all the way at her, "yes, Sir," as I'm sure that saucy minx knew it would. She used to call me that whenever she wanted me to fuck her hard.

I watch her slip her skirt and shirt on, but leave her panties, bra, and corset off. Knowing she's going to be without panties on the drive home will be agony. Yep, shower sex is happening. I'll bend her over and really make sure she's the one seeing stars this time.

I straighten up my clothes as she puts her boots on. I turn off the lights to the stockroom and we leave the building hand in hand. In the parking lot, I fill my lungs with the crisp night air, feeling alive for the first time in months. Mindy smiles at me and deep down, I know this experience has changed something for the better.

The End

About Lacey Cross

Lacey Cross is a wife sharing erotica writer with over 100 short stories published since she started in 2021. Her stories emphasize the pleasure found from the wife living her best slut life and embracing the hotwife lifestyle. She explores themes of free use, submissive wives with dominant bulls, BDSM...and oh-so-many men.